T0062972

Also by Donna Underwood

Non-fiction:
Original Loss
Original Loss Revisited
Grief Works

Fiction:
The Support Group
The Divorce Group
The Prisoner's Group

The Prisoners' Group

A MYSTERY NOVEL

Donna Underwood

abbott press

Abbott Press books may be ordered through booksellers or by contacting:

Abbott Press
1663 Liberty Drive
Bloomington, IN 47403
www.abbottpress.com
Phone: 1 (866) 697-5310

ISBN: 978-1-4582-2106-3 (sc)
ISBN: 978-1-4582-2105-6 (hc)
ISBN: 978-1-4582-2104-9 (e)

Library of Congress Control Number: 2017907661

Print information available on the last page.

Abbott Press rev. date: 06/20/2017

DEDICATED TO...

To all who have spent time in jail or prison.

To all who experienced cruelty, chaos, abuse, and insensitivity in their childhoods.

To all who were not taught to appreciate their own self-worth and who were not encouraged to work towards their innate potential.

.............and lastly to all who despite their painful childhoods have grown to be kind, loving, thoughtful adults and have helped any person or creature who needed a kind word or helping hand.

Be a cheerleader for yourself and others always.

IN APPRECIATION

My sincere appreciation to the following four people for their time, experience and encouragement.

To my husband, Wayne, for his strength of character, for making me laugh when challenges got tough and for his undying encouragement. He was kind enough to read my corrected manuscript and correct my typos....that's love!

To my editor, Patty Clark, who spent long hours correcting my many grammatical errors, of which there were plenty. Thank goodness for her unwavering patience and humor. She confessed she laughed out loud at a few of my spelling choices.

To Dr. Kris Marks, Ph.d. who kindly offered suggestions as to prison life. Her interest in the subject of my writing was one of the motivations for completing The Prisoner's Group.

To Patricia Klukkert who has years of experience working with women in jail. She kindly read the manuscript and offered valuable insights and suggestions.

My sincere appreciation to all of the four for their time, experience and encouragement. I believe there is a desperate need for the program I have written about in this book.

LIST OF MAIN CHARACTERS

Brooksie Everett: social worker, owner of Grief Clinic and facilitator in pilot program at Lancer's Women's Prison.'

Lucinda Chavez Padilla: social worker from the Grief Clinic.

Rachael Satori: social worker from the Grief Clinic.

Anita Pace: student in a Master's Program, volunteer from the Grief Clinic.

Dr. Sharon Primm: inmate. Worked at the Grief Clinic as a psychologist. Found guilty of murdering her sister.

Dr. Florence James: Warden of Lancer's Prison.

Mrs. Malina Smithers: assistant to the warden.

Dr. Mitchel Ronan, M.D: Prison's daytime physician.

Mrs. Janet Black, RN: Dr. Ronan's assistant.

The inmates attending a six month workshop in the prison: Houston, Wilamina, Delores, Jackie, Sammy, Sasha, Corrina, Charlotte, Berri, and Luella.

PROLOGUE

Why would she want to meet me in the laundry room? I was going to see her after lunch, like we planned. It doesn't make any sense.

"Damn it, where are you?" whispered Simone to herself, as she looked nervously down the row of industrial washing machines and dryers.

A barely discernible voice answered, "I'm over here at the end of the row, next to the closet."

Simone moved quickly to the location of the sound of the voice, then stopped short. *That doesn't sound like Houston. What's going on, Houston wouldn't trick me, not her. Something's not right. I gotta get out of here, run stupid, run.*

She immediately turned around and ran into the waiting, muscular arms of a man dressed in prison guard clothing. Simone opened her mouth wide to scream. Too late. Her mouth was covered by a third hand while the first attacker's hands were tightening around her young throat. She fought like a wildcat. She got a hold of someone's arm and bit into the soft flesh with all her ebbing strength. Something heavy crashed at the back of her head. The last thing she heard was a scream - not hers. She then heard someone say, "Make that bitch let go." As the pumping of her heart slowed down and eventually quit all together her last thought was, *my friends were right, this place is hell.*

CHAPTER ONE

**"You'll never be good enough for some people.
The question is, is that your problem or theirs."**
Author unknown

Workshop #1

"I'm excited and scared about presenting our first workshop today. I don't want to turn the participants off, but I sure as hell don't want to make them mad at us either," expressed Lucinda.

"I feel the same way," responded Brooksie. "My heart is racing and soon my stomach will start to act up. Most of my fear has to do with my effectiveness. Can we really make a difference in the lives of these incarcerated women? Six months isn't a very long time to offer these workshops and expect constructive change. I don't have the foggiest idea what it's like to be imprisoned. My childhood wasn't a 'leave it to Beaver' kind of scene, but it certainly wasn't filled with drugs, criminals, beatings, sexual shit and other kinds of abuses either. These women may see right through us. Like we are only do-gooders and don't have a clue what they have experienced."

"I don't know about that. You've shared your mother's four marriages, numerous school and neighborhood changes and your strong feelings of abandonment. I'll bet some of the inmates have had similar experiences, don't you think so?" questioned Lucinda.

"You're probably right. Those old abandonment feelings creep into my psyche when I least expect them. Maybe I'll learn something useful for myself as well as for the prisoners. Also I want Sharon's project to become successful and the programs to be offered to other prisons. She deserves to have her hard work bring about change for the good in all of the prisoners' lives. What's the worst thing that could happen? The program's failure to achieve any worthwhile changes in the women's behaviors; we could be beaten up and taken as hostages or maybe even murdered?" said Brooksie with a wide grin.

The two women exchanged knowing looks with each other. Lucinda turned away and began to laugh uproariously, soon joined by Brooksie. They were both still laughing as they drove into the prison's parking area.

"Do you think we will run into Loreli?" asked Lucinda.

"I hope not. In my opinion, she is a dangerous psychopath'" responded Brooksie.

They parked and walked through the several locked gates, as they had done before when they met with the Warden James. Their purses and coats were taken from them and placed in a secure area. They were permitted to carry in the workbooks and pencils that Sharon had asked them to bring. A female guard led them to the cafeteria. Sharon stood up as soon as she spotted the two friends enter.

Sharon, Brooksie and Lucinda exchanged bear hugs and greetings.

"Hope you are as excited as I am," said Sharon.

"I'm way past excited," responded Brooksie. "And I have the sweaty palms to prove it!"

"Tony sends his best wishes for a fantastic first time workshop," beamed Lucinda.

"That doesn't surprise me one bit," responded Brooksie. "He is a thoughtful and generous man. You've definitely married Mr. Right."

Sharon added, "Lucinda, you deserve a loving partner and sounds like he does too."

"You also deserve a truckload of happiness," affirmed Lucinda.

"You were sorely missed at the wedding Sharon, but we did make a toast to you later that day," added Brooksie. "This is way off the subject at hand, but did you receive a request from a Loreli Woods to join a group in your program? She would be a fairly new inmate."

"Yes I did." responded Sharon. "Anita had forewarned me about Loreli's attempt on her husband's life. She told me Mr. Woods was a member in your divorce group. I informed Loreli the groups were filled. The rumor has it that she is awaiting extradition to England in order to stand trial for the murder of another husband. She's been a busy girl. She's not in the general population here. I've only seen her one time and that was in the infirmary. She was waiting to see Dr. Ronan. Hope he has been warned about her.

A bell rang and a group of ten inmates noisily came through the cafeteria doors. They meandered toward one of the cafeteria tables where Sharon was sitting.

Sharon instructed the women to sit down at either side of the table. This was accomplished after much wrangling about who was to sit next to whom. All of a sudden, a loud alarm starts blasting off!

"My God! What's that? yelled Lucinda.

"Keep your panties on deary," said Charotte, "It's nothing to worry your pretty little head over."

A guard strolled over to the group, looked at Sharon and exclaimed, "It seems one of your cell mates is missing. A small amount of fresh blood was discovered in the laundry room. Doc, we are in lockdown. The warden told me to tell you to go ahead with your class or whatever it is you are attempting to do here. Nobody leaves this room till the all clear is given."

"Thank you Ms. White," answered Sharon. "Can you tell us the name of the missing person?"

"No. Not yet. I was told she signed up for this class, but they didn't tell me her name."

The inmates talked amongst themselves. The sound level of chatter was rapidly increasing. Charlotte's face turned ashen, as did Houston's. Two of the inmates grabbed onto each other. All of the women, including Lucinda and Brooksie, showed varying degrees of fear or anxiety. Many were wide-eyed. Both facilitators kept their eyes on Sharon. Sharon appeared calm and in charge, much to the relief of the two social workers.

"Corrina, too bad it's not your fat body that's missing, of course, nobody would miss you. Except maybe your mirror," sneered Wilamina.

"Shut up, Willy. You're just jealous 'cause you couldn't make a buck on your back," challenged Corrina.

"Ladies," Sharon said in a quiet tone, "This news of someone missing is upsetting to most of us in the room, but you will remain civil toward one another. If the majority want to cancel the meeting for today, we can do that. Remember we don't know how long we'll be here, together! Raise your hand if you want to cancel today's program."

Two inmates, Luella, (nicknamed Lu) and Berri raised their hands. They both looked at the others, seeing that they were the only ones with raised hands, lowered theirs.

"Okay. Looks like we are on for today," affirmed Sharon. "Everyone has been instructed as to the rules of conduct, but I'm going to refresh your memories. There will be no swearing, no fighting, everyone gets a turn to talk, no one leaves the room unless nature calls. You will then be accompanied to the rest room by Ms. White.

"Today I'm an observer. Ms. Padilla and Ms. Everett are your instructors. There will be a sixty minute workshop and sixty minutes to discuss, share and ask questions. This group will meet every other Wednesday at 9:30 a.m. until 11:30 a.m. This is a pilot program. The goal is to give each one of you tools to improve your lives while you call this place your home, as well as when you are released. You can drop out. If you choose to drop out, you will not be permitted to attend other workshops for the next six months.

Brooksie began, "I appreciate that you all are wearing name tags. Unlike my coworker Lucinda, I have a hard time remembering names. Lucinda is passing out a questionnaire and a pencil for each of you. Please do not put your name on the questionnaire. We will collect these before you leave today. If you would like a copy of the questionnaire for yourselves, pick one up as you leave the room. I'm going to read the questions out loud, in case anyone has a question.

- Best memory of childhood?
- Worst memory of childhood?
- Happiest time of childhood?
- Best friend?
- What do you consider your best trait, best skill and favorite activity?
- Who do you blame for your incarceration?
- Meaningful losses in your life? (deaths, injuries, illnesses, abandonment, freedom, friendships, partners, health, home, job, trust, self-respect and others)"

Brooksie addressed the guard, "Ms. White would you like to fill out your own?"

"Why not. Might learn something about my own glorious life," she answered.

"Please take the next ten minutes to answer these questions. One side is English and the other side, Spanish." informed Lucinda. *Thinking to herself, it's a good thing Sharon made sure all participants could read and write in English or Spanish.*

After ten minutes was up, Lucinda asked, "Since this is the first session, we are not starting out with a workshop theme. Brooksie and I would like to get to know you better. Would anyone be willing to volunteer to share what they wrote?"

Houston raised her hand first. "I've nothing to lose. My best memory was a puppy mama gave me. I was a little tyke of three years old or maybe I was five. My worst memory, daddy killed the puppy, 'cause he said the pup messed on the floor. Happiest time was with my Nana. She baked cookies just for me. She even held me sometimes when I cried. Worst time ever was when she died.

"I'm not sure what a trait is, but I'm real loyal. It's my loyalty that got me arrested the first time. My favorite activity is cooking chili and playing pool. I'm real good at both. Someday I hope to have another puppy.

"I checked off all the losses, except the health one. I'm still okay, never been really sick. Broke some bones in my face and wrist, running into several of my boyfriends fists, at different times. Once in a while, I sent a few of them to the emergency room. They was too embarrassed to say a female had beat them up." She exchanged a knowing look with others. Muffled snickering could be heard from a few.

"My best friend was Annabelle. We went off in different directions. Sometimes there wasn't enough for me to eat. Annabelle shared her lunch with me. When we were in the same school. We didn't have much of a house. Not enough room for three brothers, me, mom and sometimes dad. Often there was just some stranger, some guy mom brought home. I didn't always get to school. Dad was arrested many times for beating mom or someone else. One of mom's boyfriend's messed with me when I was young, about six or seven years old. All in all, mom did her best. She had a lot of bad luck. She'd bring any jerk home. The last guy was the worst. One day he went crazy. He started to choke her. Her face was turning blue and she had quit fighting back. I hit him with a frying pan over and over. He wouldn't let her go. Then I hit him as hard as I could, same pan. He finally stopped and went down. I'm not proud of what I did, but I had to save her. Later on she blamed me for killing that piece of shit. She told the police I went insane. She was stinking drunk and I don't think she even remembers he was choking her to death. Her neck looked like she has been hanging from a rope. The police believed her, not me. She's not okay in the head, too much booze and crack. I don't blame her. She don't know any better. That's all I wrote.

"Huston, thanks for sharing. You did a good job and this helps us to get to know you a little better. I appreciate your honesty and especially your willingness to go first," expressed Brooksie.

Next, Wilamina raised her hand and blurted out, "I'm next." She looked at Houston and said, "We could be sisters, except I'm black and you're real pale and blonde. Made me sad to hear what you wrote 'cause it's like my life. Want me to read mine teacher?" looking at Brooksie.

"Yes," answered Brooksie. "Please, do and call me Brooksie. Everyone in this room is a teacher. We can all learn from each other. Go ahead Wilamina."

A few of the inmates laughed and Wilamina said, "They're laughing at my name, around here I'm called Willy."

"Do you want us to call you Willy or Wilamina? asked Brooksie.

"I like hearing my real name so Wilamina is okay with me. Let'm laugh. I can't think of a good memory, but I got lots of bad ones. Guess my worst one was the time mama's boyfriend nearly beat her to death. I was five, maybe six years old. I tried to stop him so I bit his leg and he threw me halfway across the room. He hurt mama's head so bad she couldn't talk or walk okay ever again. Then grandma had to take care of me, my two brothers and ma. She did what she could, but she was old and tired and could barely get around herself. She was all crippled up with the aches.

"I can't say nothing about happy times just hard times. Jerome, my older brother died in a car crash. He was seventeen. Royal, the youngest, kinda got lost on drugs. I still think about Jerome. He tried to take care of me and Royal. I was thirteen when he died.

"My friend Shana hurt me bad. She stole money from me several times. I wasn't smart enough to catch on. Guess she needed her dope more'n our friendship. It was her boyfriend who finally ratted her out about stealing from me, 'cause he got mad at her for cheating on him. Bothers me just to talk about Shana."

"Thanks Wilamina for sharing what you could. It took courage to share what you did." added Lucinda. "Do we have another volunteer?

'"Okay. I can do it. You said not to put our name on this, right?" asked Charlotte.

"That's right, Charlotte," responded Lucinda, looking at Charlotte's name tag.

"You can call me Char, if you want to. Everybody does. My best memory was a Christmas. I was seven. My dad, mom, brother and sister were there. We had presents, a tree, a nice dinner and even sang songs.

"My worst memory was the next Christmas because my baby sister was in the hospital and died after a few days. Our house was never the same. Eventually dad left us. Never saw him again.

Mom worked hard and long hours to pay the bills. There were many tough times.

"My happiest time was because Jackson and I got together. I was seventeen years old. He made me laugh. We had some real good times, but he couldn't seem to hold onto a job for longer than a few months. I started working two jobs and he stopped working all together. We needed money, owed every one. He convinced me to help him rob a liquor store. I was only going to drive the car and he would go inside and demand the money. Stupid, lazy Jackson took a gun in, so happens the owner also had a gun. Jackson was shot dead. Here I am for the next fifteen or twenty years. Oh, yeah, I checked off all the losses and added loss of hope and future."

"Thanks Charlotte for your willingness to help us to know a little about your story. Perhaps you will gain hope for your future by the end of our six months," remarked Brooksie.

"Okay. I'll go next," said Corrina. "My worst memory was the death of my baby. I was sixteen and so happy because Jose was happy. We got married in church before she was even born. I don't know what went wrong, but she died a few hours after she was born. I never got to hold her. My 'abuella' told me it was God's punishment. Jose also blamed me and told me his mother said I was a bad girl. His family accused me of tricking Jose into getting me pregnant. My parents had seven other kids and told me to find a job and another place to live. They were ashamed of me and told me so many times.

"Jose divorced me with the church's blessing. I could never get pregnant again. Believe me, I tried with a bunch of other guys, but no baby.

"I put an X by all the losses. I'm a diabetic, have Herpes and high blood pressure. I'm also fat. Never had enough food as a kid.

Never had enough of anything. At least in here you're not too hot or too cold, have your own bed and food three times a day."

"Thanks Corrina for sharing a part of your story. I'm sorry about the loss of your baby, but also for the unwarranted blame thrown on you by the adults," said Brooksie.

"You had your hand up Berri. Would you like to go next?" asked Brooksie.

"Yes." responded Berri. "I lost two babies. My first one died 'bout a week after being born. She was a girl. My second baby was a son. Ali, was only ten months old and my ex-boyfriend beat him because he wouldn't stop crying. My Ali died same day in the hospital. I was working and Sam, my boyfriend was supposed to be taking care of Ali. He threw my baby against the f...... wall. I made sure Sam paid. I poisoned him. He died crying out in pain, just like my Ali. I'm not one bit sorry about Sam. I think about Ali every day. Hope he's waiting for me.

"My best memory and happiest time was with my grandpa when I was little girl. He took me fishing at the beach. He laughed a lot and made me laugh. He drank too much, but he was good to me. I still miss him and Ali. Ali was the cutest little guy you ever did see. I got a picture of him in my cell.

"I checked off everything about the losses. I have high blood pressure. I could drop a few pounds. Never had a house, always in some dumpy apartment. Moved a lot with my ma, that is when she was around. She worked the streets at night. I was always scared at night alone."

One by one the inmates, continued to share their answers to the questionnaire, until most of the first hour was used up. "Our first hour has gone by quickly. Let's take a five minute break," said Sharon.

A few of the inmates asked to go to the restroom. Ms. White, the CO, accommodated their requests. Sharon and the facilitators moved to another table away from earshot of the remaining participants.

Brooksie asked, "How do you think this is going Sharon?"

"Better than I expected. They all seem comfortable answering the questions. If we remain in lock-up mode at 11:30 we can take advantage and use that extra time to ask for questions and comments. Just as a side note I believe the missing inmate is Simone. She signed up for this workshop. Simone has been acting differently the last month or so. Something was bothering her. I hope she is soon found safe and sound."

CHAPTER TWO

"When you know better, you do better."
Maya Angelou (1928-2014)

Workshop #1 continued....

The three chatted for a few more minutes and then returned to the group table.

"There are still five ladies that need time to share their responses to the questions." announced Lucinda. "Anyone willing to begin?"

"I didn't have a crappy childhood, like many others," began Delores."My Dad worked the same job, Mom took care of me and my brothers. I was a good student and became an R.N. I worked in the emergency room for a few years. My two brothers were in a terrible car accident. Rick, the oldest died and Dan, the youngest was seriously injured. Dan was the driver. He has had chronic back and neck pain ever since. He eventually got hooked on his pain medication and went on to become addicted to many illegal and legal drugs.

"In the meantime, I'd fallen in love with an intern, Carlos. We started on drugs in social settings, but quickly lost control. One thing led to another. I lost my job. Carlos was doing badly at the hospital in the intern program. Carlos, Dan and I began stealing for drug money and finally our luck ran out and here I am.

"My best time was graduation day from nursing school. Worst time was getting lost in the world of drugs and committing crimes to support the habit.

"My parents are devastated. They never got over the death of their first and favorite child. Still, they didn't deserve to have Dan and myself become addicts and criminals. My folks are decent and hard working. I got lost. What started as recreational relaxation became the end of the road for me, Carlos and Dan.

"Some of these women here have had terrible beginnings. No wonder they became so self-destructive. I have no excuses, only can blame myself. My losses are self-respect, health problems including bad teeth, two brothers, one boyfriend and the love of my parents. The worst is the hurt I've caused my folks and what I've done to myself. Even Dan has more of an excuse than I do. I had a good life going and I threw it all away."

"Could I go next?" asked Sammy. "This is beginning to get depressing. I'm here because I beat my partner almost to death. I wanted to be a veterinarian, but I made poor grades in school and had little money. I was the only kid my folks could have. My mom was domineering and mean as a dog in heat. My Dad drove a taxi and worked long hours. Mom complained all the time about everything. She was a first class bitch.

"I'm gay. I kept it a secret from my folks until my thirties. They were both horrified, especially Mom. We haven't spoken in over twenty years.

"I've worked as a cook, bus driver and veterinarian's assistant. When I was thirty-five I had a good job with a vet. I owned three great dogs, had a fine partner. Her name is Louny. She had some issues. She was bi-polar and couldn't stay on her medications. One morning we had a terrible argument and I left to go to work. She went crazy and tortured and killed two of my beloved dogs. I think she was jealous of my pets. She called me at work and sounded hysterical. She screamed at me and said I better get home if I wanted to see my dogs again. I raced home to find two of my beloved pets bloody, broken and dead. Ramrod, the St. Bernard was bleeding but he survived. I lost it. I beat Louny with my bare hands. Thought I'd killed her. Finally got myself under control, called for an ambulance. Louny was taken to the hospital and I drove my precious dog to the vet. I hurt Louny so bad and now she is paralyzed from the waist down. The doc had to put Ramrod down. I loved that big dog. I turned myself in to the police after I buried my pets."

Brooksie wiped her eyes and said, "I'm sorry your partner was mentally ill and took out her confused feelings on your innocent and precious pets. I have dogs and cats and know how attached I am to them. Violent deaths of the innocent, humans or animals, are hard to understand, to make peace with and to grieve."

"My name is Sasha. My father is black and my mother was Japanese. My father is serving a life term and mother is dead. They were both drug dealers, hired mules to bring in stuff from Mexico. I began to work for them when I was thirteen years old. Police raided our place. Dad killed a cop, a cop killed Mom, I injured a cop. I think it was my friend Ling So that turned us in. Friends and family just don't turn each other in. Bad karma. The day of the raid was my worst day. I can't think of a best day. Maybe I will learn about being happy in this class. But, I won't hold my breath."

"Sasha, I'm sorry about the death of your mother, but I feel worse about the childhood you had," responded Lucinda.

"You don't have to feel sorry for me. I'm young and have many good years left," said Sasha as she gave Lucinda a penetrating stare.

"You don't have to worry about Sasha. She's tough and can take care of herself," said Luella. "I was doing okay until my husband got injured when we worked in the fields. He got in a car accident. We were involved in the gang life. My mama not too smart. She quit school real early, she couldn't read very good. My papa and I took care of her. I don't know what's happening to her now. My best time was when I was a little girl. I played with my cousins and neighbors. Worst time started at thirteen and only got worse. I've been addicted to everything I could swallow, snort or shoot. My health is lousy and I'm only twenty-five years old. My babies were taken away. My papa is heart-broken. I don't see any future for me."

"Luella, sometimes only looking ahead one hour is far enough future for the time being. There are baby steps you can take that will get you to the next hour, next day and eventually the next week." said Brooksie.

"Looks like I'm the last one," said Jackie. "It's no secret. I'm also gay and so is my younger brother, Kent. My older brother, Darion, is a minister and tells Kent and me all the time that we are going to hell. My parents have money. That is a big part of their problems. My father is an English Professor at a university. My mother's name is Ashley Winkler. Her family are the owners of a well-known company called Ashley Cosmetics. They have the big money and status. My happiest memories are time with my nanny. She basically raised me. I loved Ms. Slauson and she loved me, and still does. I realized 'bout the time I turned thirteen I was interested in girls, not boys. I think Ms. Slauson knew this before I did. She never judged me. I have many more bad memories than good ones. Kent, is a hypocrite and ass kisser. He comes to visit me sometimes. Darion, the bible thumper, never comes to see me." Jackie let out a long, low sigh and became quiet.

Brooksie thanked Jackie then addressed the group, while Lucinda collected the pencils. "Lucinda and I both sincerely appreciate your participation in this pilot program. Neither one of us have any idea what it is like to be incarcerated, so we appreciate any and all of your insights, suggestions and criticisms. Our hope is for you to recognize and understand your past situations and what they have to do with your present situation. Our goal is to help you change and improve your future."

Sharon spoke up to all present, "Our two hours group work session is over. We are going to stay here in the cafeteria until the lunch meal is ready. Ms. White, are Ms. Everett and Ms. Padilla able to leave now?"

"The all-clear has not yet been given, so we are all to stay put for now, even the guests," responded the guard.

Several of the inmates asked the guard if she would escort them to the rest room. Ms. White led three out the door to the restroom.

Sharon led Brooksie and Lucinda to a corner table, away from the group of inmates. "This first session went very well, in my opinion," said Sharon. "How do the two of you feel about it?"

"I learned just how common poverty, domestic abuse, lack of education, numerous losses, especially of hope has played in their lives. Most of their stories made me angry and extremely sad." responded Brooksie.

"I feel the same way, " answered Lucinda. Many of them have experienced nightmarish childhoods. I'm pleasantly surprised how willing they were to talk about themselves."

The entire group remained in 'locked-down' for the next two hours. Several of the inmates visited with the facilitators and asked a few personal questions concerning marriage, boyfriends and children. A few elaborated more on their own personal stories. For the most part, the group seemed relaxed and even enjoyed the conversations. Houston appeared distracted and chose not to join in any of the conversations.. Sharon kept glancing over her shoulder at her.

CHAPTER THREE

**"Always do right.
This will gratify some people
and astonish the rest."**
Mark Twain (Samuel L. Clemens)1835-1910

Dr James, came through the cafeteria doors walking briskly. She was accompanied by two guards. She addressed Sharon and her two facilitators. "I'm sorry your partners were detained. They will be escorted back to the gates now. Ms. Everett and Mrs. Padilla please follow these two guards. My apology again for the delay."

Brooksie and Lucinda quickly hugged Sharon and thanked her for the opportunity to be on the ground floor of such a fine project. In unison they said their good-bye's to the inmates. Brooksie added, "We'll see you in two weeks. Thanks for your spirit of cooperation and meaningful participation."

Dr. James remained in the cafeteria. "I have some disturbing news to share. I thought it best to wait until the two outsiders left before telling you Simone has been found unconscious. We found her hidden in a closet, covered with dirty laundry. She's been badly beaten and her condition is grave. Dr. Ronan is with her now, awaiting the ambulance."

Houston's face paled and she begged, "She can't be left alone with that doctor. She could be in danger. Please!"

"Calm yourself, Houston," said the warden. "Dr. Ronan will take care of her until she can be transported. I can see how upset you are, but the doctor isn't the one who hurt Simone."

Corrina moved quickly next to Houston. Put her arms around her and whispered into her ear. Houston tried to push her away, but Corrina held her tight and said, "She'll be okay. Simone is her friend." She was addressing the Warden.

"Do you know who attacked Simone?" asked Sharon, looking at the Warden.

"Not yet. I'm hoping she'll be able to identify her attacker, when she becomes conscious. I'll pass on any updates I receive. I notified the authorities. Detective Yomoto called back immediately and we'll meet together today and get a report started."

The cafeteria began to fill with hungry and noisy inmates. After a two hour delay, Lunch was finally available.

Sharon maneuvered her way over next to Houston. "Would you join me over there against the wall? Where it is a bit quieter?"

Corrina asked if she could join them. Houston answered, "Maybe later."

When they settled themselves, Sharon said, "We are out of earshot of the others, what is going on?"

Houston responded, "Guess I have to trust someone besides Mela, the night nurse. Might as well be you. Dr. Ronan is bad news. So is, Janet Black, the day nurse. She kisses his ass daily and turns a blind eye to his shitty deeds. I swear the man is stealing drugs right from under the Warden's nose. I don't know if she's just stupid, pretends ignorance or truly just doesn't know what's going on. Dr. Ronan can't be working alone. He must have helpers besides the nurse. When someone goes to sick bay and needs something for pain, some are given sugar pills and others get the "real mc coy". I know the difference, trust me.

"Does anyone else share your opinion about Dr. Ronan?" inquired Sharon. "Do you have any proof?"

"A few months ago Simone twisted her ankle real bad. It was swollen black and blue. She could barely walk on it. She went to the infirmary, and was examined by Dr. Ronan. He felt up more than her injured ankle. She told me she was afraid to tell him to stop. The doc told her that is was too bad he didn't have more time, but he had another inmate waiting. He gave her some pills for pain, the envelope read Tylenol/Codeine. They didn't relieve shit. They did absolutely nothing for her!. She was supposed to go back, but she didn't.

"I still have the pills and I want to get them taken to the outside to be tested. Can you do it. Can you get the pills to an outside lab without this place knowing anything about it?"

Sharon's throat felt as dry as the desert in summer and her hands were trembling. She answered, "Next week there will be two new facilitators here to start their program with a different group of inmates. Get the pills to me and I'll see that Rachael and Anita take them to a reputable lab. I sure hope you're not simply going stir crazy and seeing problems that don't exist."

"Trust me doc," said Houston. "Simone found out something this morning that someone (or more than someone) didn't want her to know. I saw her at breakfast and she looked horrified. She gave me a hand signal to meet her after lunch in the rec. room. I believe she was beaten because of what she had found out. She is a fine young person. She doesn't belong in prison. Simone is kind and has a trusting nature. She must have accidentally discovered something that put her in danger and now I'm involving you. I'm sorry about that doc, I really am. You've been treating us good." Houston lowered her head and looked away.

"You can trust me, Houston. I take your accusations seriously. Cautiously slip the pills to me as soon as you can. My friends from the Grief Clinic will see they are tested. We'd better join the others now."

Houston leaned in close to Sharon and in whisper said, "Don't trust anyone except maybe the night nurse Mela Washingon. She seems straight."

Later that day.........

The inmates were gathered in the cafeteria for dinner time. The Warden walked in and made an announcement. "I'm sorry to have to inform you of this sad news, but Simone has died. She never regained consciousness. We will find out who is responsible for her death. I give you my word, the attacker will not go undiscovered for long. Everyone who had any opportunity to attack Simone will be called to my office. I believe that there will be quite a few of you. This will take some time. I expect your full your cooperation and patience during our investigation. Detective Yomoto and Detective Rowe will conduct most of the interviews that they deem necessary. These will include staff and inmates as well."

Sounds of muffled crying and whispering could be heard throughout the large room. Houston spoke out in a loud booming voice, "I'll find out who did this and you know who you are, you are going to pay."

The infirmary was busy all day and into the evening hours. Dr. Gibran took over the duties at 6 p.m. from Dr. Ronan. "I understand the inmate Simone died today from a beating and the perpetrator is still unknown as of yet."

Dr. Ronan responded, "Yes. A very unfortunate thing to happen to such a young and pretty woman. Hopefully they'll quickly find out who was responsible. I'm off and glad of it. It's been a long day. Hope you have an uneventful evening."

"Weren't you treating Simone, a while back, Mitchel?" asked Dr. Gibran.

"I remember she was young and attractive, but I don't recall what her problems were, I see so many patients every day, no way could I file away each one's specific conditions. See you later."

"I didn't mean to suggest you remember each patient and their diagnosis. Have a good evening." Dr. Gibran thought, *he seems rather defensive tonight and is perspiring excessively. Guilty conscience maybe?"*

By 9 p.m. Dr. Gibran was finally taking a much needed break. She spoke to the evening nurse, "Mela, don't we usually see more patients at night than Dr. Ronan does on his shift?"

"Yes, doc, but I think they like you better. Dr. Ronan makes me uncomfortable. The way he looks at the younger inmates gives me a bad feeling," answered the nurse.

"Oh Mela, he's a man and most men stare at young women. That's in their genes, get it? Jeans."

"Nice play on words doc. Maybe you're right, but these young women are vulnerable and he represents power and control. He can easily take advantage of his position."

There was a knock on the clinic's door. "Come in." said Mela.

"Am I too late? I don't feel so good. My hand and arm are really hurting. Dr. Ronan treated me earlier today, but I'm feeling worse," said the inmate.

"What is your name?" asked the nurse.

"I'm Maxine Ritter."

"Come closer and let me take a look," said Dr. Gibran. The doctor removed the dressing as the nurse placed a thermometer under Maxine's tongue and she proceeded to take her blood pressure.

Next Mela left the room to get Maxine's chart from the file. When she returned, she removed the thermometer from Maxine's mouth and stated, "You have a temp of 101 degrees. Dr. Ronan wrote down that he gave you an injection of antibiotics and some pain pills, didn't they help with the discomfort?"

"Shit no. They did nothing. I've taken six pills and still nothing."

"How did this injury happen?" inquired the doctor. "This here looks like a bite mark."

"I fell down and landed on something with sharp edges. I've always been a bit clumsy. No ballet lessons for me." Maxine smiled and let out a chuckle.

Dr. Gibran stated, "This is infected. You must come back tomorrow morning, get another antibiotic injection and have the wound cleaned every day for the next week, and take these antibiotics, one three times a day till gone. If you notice any red lines forming near the wound, come to the clinic no matter what time, day or night. Do you understand? Mela will give you some other pain pills to be taken every six hours."

"Thanks doc. I'll do whatever you say." She left the clinic and Mela closed the door behind Maxine and asked, "Again another complaint about the pain meds not helping? And I've got to say, I think she was lying about how she got hurt. Her explanation sounded weird."

"I'm sure that was a bite mark," responded Dr. Gibran. "I'm going to find out more about the injuries and the death of inmate Simone."

"You and I know there have been complaints about the pain medications not relieving discomfort, for a long time now. I've got to say it again I get a creepy feeling about Dr. Ronan. There is something about his eyes, they're shifty. Janet, his nurse acts protective of him. I'll bet my measly wage she has a possessive crush on him."

"For your information only, I'm keeping detailed notes on patients and keeping them at home. I chart less on the files that are kept here in this office," said Dr. Gibran.

"I've been doing the same thing, doc, and keep my notes at home as well. Guess we need to keep this just between us for now."

CHAPTER FOUR

**"Our deeds determine us, as much as we
determine our deeds."**
George Eliot, *Adam Bede*

Homicide investigation

Warden James notified the police department of the apparent murder of Simone Floure immediately after the body had been discovered. She met with Detective Jerry Yomoto and his partner Detective Kalie Rowe at the hospital. A second meeting was scheduled for that afternoon.

That morning, Warden James spoke briefly to Janet Black.

"Hello Mrs. Black. Thank you for coming to my office on such short notice."

"I'm not sure why I'm here," responded Janet.

"The police are investigating the death of Simone Flourre and I wanted to ask if you have any information that they might find useful in finding the perpetrator?"

"Why would you think I know anything about her death?" questioned Janet, with her usual uppity tone.

"I'm aware Simone visited the clinic, in the past, and has been seen by Dr. Ronan. Since you are his long-time nurse, I assumed you know different things about the patients he has treated."

Janet squirmed in her chair and picked at something invisible on her starched uniform. "The good doctor attends to many patients every day. Surely I'm not expected to remember every inmate and what they're seen for."

"No, of course not, but that is the reason for keeping records of visits, treatments and the reasons for the visits. When we are done here I will follow you back to the clinic and you will be kind enough to pull the charts for Simone and Maxine Ritter. By the way, when Dr. Ronan sees any female patients for any sort of examination, are you always present in the exam room with him?"

Janet became more visibly agitated. She crossed and uncrossed her right leg over her left several times. Her voice was becoming higher pitch and she began talking faster. "My job requires my presence in the exam room when the patient is a female, unless the patient herself requests privacy. Doctor Ronan has told me repeatedly that everyone has a right to keep a secret or two. The charts are confidential. I'm sure you know all about the Privacy Act, so I won't say more. I do not want to be accused of anything illegal. I certainly hope our integrity is not being questioned here."

"Did I infer anyone's integrity was in question?"

Janet said to the Warden, "You know how inmates talk. They will lie first and only tell the truth if it benefits them in some way. We both know how rumors fly through this prison. Dr. Ronan is a very attractive man. Some of the inmates seem to fantasize about him."

"Do you find Dr. Ronan attractive, Janet? The two of you have been working together for more than three years. Things happen even to the best of people in stressful conditions, most not planned. Heaven only knows that the prison environment can be a very stressful place, especially over a long term."

Janet's blush began on her neck area and quickly engulfed her entire face. She stammered a few words, "We are both married and the good doctor is too much of a gentleman to do anything out of line. We are professional friends."

"So you never socialize outside of the prison?"

"Never." answered Janet. "Dr. Ronan said that would be unprofessional."

"Thanks, Janet, for talking with me. Now I will accompany you back to the clinic so you can hand those two files over to me."

Janet suggested that they should meet at a more convenient time, when there was less of a patient load. The Warden said it would only take a minute for her to go to the filing cabinet and pull the two files herself, in order to save time for her busy staff.

The crimson blush on Janet's face was replaced by a blanching of color. They walked down the hall with Dr. James in the lead and Janet walking with her head down looking like a steer heading for the slaughter house.

Later..........

The Warden had made a quick call to Detective Yomoto and suggested he bring two warrants for the files of Miss Flourre and Ms. Ritter, and if possible add warrants for all charts of females under the age of twenty-five, names unknown at this time.

I don't have to be a mind reader to see that Janet is infatuated with the 'good doctor'. I wonder just how far she would go to protect his reputation. It would be interesting to be a mouse in the corner of Janet's home and in the clinics examining room when occupied. Dr. Ronan is in perfect position to abuse his license. Wish I know the state of their marriages.

The afternoon meeting..........

The two detectives were shown to the warden's office by a prison CO.

"Thank you for coming so quickly," said Dr. James to the detectives. She brought them up to date on the facts of the murder case of Simone.

Detective Rowe showed the warden the two warrants she asked for. "We could not obtain the other warrants you asked for without names and just cause. The presiding judge is a real stickler for the law."

The three looked over the files the warden had commandeered from the nurse. They agreed, the notes scribbled by Dr. Ronan said very little except that antibiotics and Oxycontin were prescribed for both Maxine and Simone given to them by Janet Black. There was little written about what the meds were actually treating. Simone's chart stated a complete exam was done and the patient needed to return to the clinic because of an ankle injury and fever. Apparently, the patient never returned for a follow-up visit. Descriptions of wounds, injuries or any kind of diagnosis were not noted on either inmates charts.

"Maxine Ritter, on the other hand, was a regular visitor to the clinic." stated Detective Rowe as she continued to read, "for various infections in different areas, plus migraine headaches and back pain were the repeated diagnoses. Oxycontin and Hydrocodeine medications were routinely ordered."

Warden James commented, "I noticed today when I was in the clinic getting these two charts, there were four young inmates waiting to see the doctor. I know three of them have had addiction challenges. Perhaps I'm becoming overly suspicious, since I've found out how little I know about the goings on at my own prison. Is there a way you can get your hands on other charts of the young women?"

Detective Yamota offered, "At the moment no, because we don't have the necessary warrants. We don't want to shoot ourselves in the shoe."

"That's shoot ourselves in the foot," corrected his partner.

"Oh sorry, I'm still learning the slang, and even after twenty years I still don't get it right. We can pick these four ladies "at random" for interviews along with many others.

"Dr. James, we have been receiving a few complaints from former inmates after their release or by the relatives of some still incarcerated. We've been gathering information for the past six months. We've had to keep you in the dark to make certain you were not part of the problem."

Warden James clutched her white knuckled hands together and her respirations quickened. "I'm horrified to think I've missed the signs of apparent abuses on my watch. I thought I was doing okay, obviously not. What can I do to help you with this investigation?"

Detective Yomoto laid out the department's plans. "For starters, We want a list of all the people that had access to Simone the day she died. Next, we will interview them. They may lead us to others to interview. Now I'm going to tell you something you need to know. The department has an informant here in your midst. I cannot identify the person just yet. We have found that once someone knows about the identity of the informant, they have trouble acting normal around that said person."

"My God, have I been sleeping at the helm for such a long time? Do I need to resign my position or what?"

"Absolutely not." returned Detective Rowe. "You have a fine record. It's important to the investigation that you carry out your normal routine. Your position and observations are key to helping us find out who the responsible people for the murder and other illegal activities going on here."

"You will be able to reach us at any hour or if we are tied up. Two other detectives will cover for us. This goes for seven days a week 24 hours a day. I've written their names and phone numbers on this paper for you in case we're unavailable. Any questions?"

"Are any of the staff or inmates in any danger at this time?"

"We don't believe so. At least not anymore than they already have been. Our informant is in a good position to warn us if problems escalate," responded the Detective. "We were made aware of the inmates receiving placebos for a variety of pain complaints several months ago. Sorry about keeping you in the dark. But, now you can see for yourself what a good job you are doing. You discovered the phony meds without our help!"

"The ones who actually deserve the credit are one of the inmates as well as the social workers. They made the discovery and brought the news to me."

"Yes they do and so do you. You are the first prison in this state to allow a six month pilot program to help individuals learn to make better choices and how to go about it."

They said their goodbyes. The warden slipped the paper with the phone numbers of the other two detectives into her pocket. *Hope I'm up for all of this cloak and dagger stuff.*

The Detectives...............

Back in their car, the detectives were driving to the precinct. Detective Rowe asked her partner, "When do you plan to let the Warden know the identity of our undercover inmate?"

"Not till I'm sure of the Warden's acting ability and exactly where her loyalties lie. Ideally, I'd like to let inmate Sharon Primm know, since she would be in a better position to assist our planted inmate. Contact between the two of them wouldn't seem so unusual or raise suspicion. Sharon already has more access to the warden than our plant because of the pilot program.

"I also believe that Houston could be another good go-between, and maybe even the night doctor and her nurse. We are still going to need someone on the weekends who can contact us if an emergency arises."

"What about the chaplain? She has a pristine record and a heart for helping," suggested Detective Rowe.

"Good idea Rowe, why don't you do a little checking around and when you're satisfied make contact with her and her home church."

"Will do boss. Your wish is my command."

"I only wish that was true," said Yamoto with a twinkle in his eyes.

CHAPTER FIVE

"A Leader is a dealer in hope."
Napoleon Bonaparte (1769-1821)

The workshop facilitators meet for lunch.....

Rachael asked, "We are anxious to hear how you got along with your first workshop. Anita and I start tomorrow and would appreciate some feedback. I've got to admit we both have a little anxiety over the inmates reactions to you."

Brooksie began, "I was thrilled to find the inmates cooperative and even eager to participate. They answered most of what we asked on the questionnaires. Everyone, with one exception, experienced tough childhoods. The stories made me sad, angry and amazed they hadn't become serial killers. Lucy may have other opinions and ideas, but poverty, addictions, abusive, neglectful parents and lack of any positive support, emotional or physical, were the common threads I heard through their stories. What's your take Lucy?"

"I agree with you, Brooksie. I would also add a lack of education and absence of goals and hope. Sharon silently observed the group's participation and when the three of us had a few minutes out of ear shot, from the inmates, she said she was pleased with the women's willingness to share so much about their personal lives.

"We did have some excitement. Because an inmate was missing, loud alarms went off. We weren't allowed to leave the grounds for several hours, later than we had planned. Later that day Sharon called Brooksie and informed her the inmate had been discovered savagely beaten. She died later.

"One more thing pertaining to the backgrounds of the ladies," added Brooksie. "It didn't sound like many of the women had ever been treated by anyone as if they counted for something worthwhile. They have no sense of their own self-worth. Respect of any kind seems foreign to them. Our workshop can do much to help these lost spirits and damaged bodies. I'm excited now more than ever about what good change can come about because of Sharon's vision and hard work."

"You know how much I think of Sharon. This doesn't surprise me to hear what great changes she will bring about for those in prison. I feel so fortunate we are getting to assist her. She's my hero." said Anita with all her white, straight teeth showing and grinning ear to ear.

"By the way," added Lucinda, "Loreli Woods, the Grief Clinic's black widow, asked to attend the pilot program. Sharon informed her the groups were all filled up. "We had given Sharon a heads up on Loreli a while back. She was aware of Loreli's attempt on her husband, Jason who was attending a divorce group at the clinic. Sharon told us Loreli is locked up twenty-three out of twenty-four hours a day. She is basically isolated from the general population. Apparently she is awaiting extradition to England to stand trial for murdering her first husband. The clinic has certainly had its share of vicious criminals. Hope a milder group of folks sign up to attend from now on."

"If you girls don't mind, I'd like to get to the important stuff," said Rachael. "How is married life, Lucy?"

"I've never been happier. I swear if the inmates had been treated as wonderfully as Tony treats me, most of the cells would be empty."

"I can't agree more," affirmed Brooksie. Luke makes me feel like I'm the greatest female on the planet. He is a fantastic, selfless cheer leader. A calm ocean with the potential of great strength. I'm a better person when I'm with him."

"So when do we look for our bridesmaid's outfits?" asked Rachael.

"Don't plan any shopping trips tomorrow, Rachael," answered Brooksie with a sweet smile, corners of her mouth turned up.

The four friends visited a while longer, sharing personal news and eventually went their separate ways.

Brooksie drove to the Grief Clinic's office to do some catch up on paper work. *I'm glad I'm going to see Luke tomorrow. He welcomes life with open arms while I'm so damn cautious. He is so different from Marino. He gives me room to breathe.*

CHAPTER SIX

"The living moment is everything."
D.H. Lawrence (1885-1930)

Brooksie stopped at the market after she finished at the office. She had invited Luke and his four year old adopted son, Drake for dinner. Once home, and after all the ritual pet greetings she jumped into the shower, then quickly dressed in Levis, a turtle neck sweater and tennis shoes. She pulled her hair into a pony tail, dabbed on lipstick and heard barking. *My great doggie alarms. Luke must be here.*

She opened the door. "Hi Luke, and who is this handsome little guy following you?"

"You know me. I'm Drake."

"Drake who?"

"Drake Jones."

He immediately sat on the floor so three dogs and two cats could give him some wet loving.

"It still tugs at my heart to hear him call me daddy and give his new last name. You sure look nice tonight. Here is the fish, Drake and I caught last week. What can I do to help with dinner?"

"Would you mind lighting the fire pit? I thought we could barbeque the fish you two caught. We can also throw on some corn on-the-cob. Drake told me that's one of his favorites. He can help me wrap up the corn in foil."

"Yeah. I do it good." squealed Drake.

After dinner, they all carried in their dirty dishes to the sink. Luke bellowed, "How about a game of badminton before it gets too dark?"

"Brooksie and me against daddy."

"You're on peewee." responded Luke.

"You've got yourself a partner little guy," chimed in Brooksie. She looked at Luke, displaying a big smile. "I hope we won't see a grown man cry when he loses."

Drake turned his serious face to her and stated, "Daddy only cries when I get 'dopted. He don't cry playing games."

Brooksie leaned down and gave Drake a big hug. "You are such a little wise person and you make me smile outside and inside."

Half an hour later after serious competition and tons of whoops and hollers, Luke begrudgingly admitted defeat. Drake jumped into his dad's arms howling, "we won, we won."

Luke trying to model good sportsmanship said, "Yes you did. You won fair and square. I congratulate you both."

Brooksie was still panting from the exertion of the game, "You gave us a good run for our money. Glad to see you're not pouting."

Luke whispered in her ear, "Next time I keep score." A wicked smile crossed his face which accentuated his dimples. "Are you free this coming Saturday night for an adult night out. My folks asked to take Drake for the night. He loves to be with them 'cause they spoil him like crazy."

"You're not just angling for a badminton rematch are you? You think I can't beat you without my wise little partner?"

Luke's eyes twinkled and he replied," Are you afraid to try it alone without your peewee assistant?

"You're on mister. What time?"

"I'll pick you up at 5 p.m. dress casually and wear shoes you can walk a short distance in."

CHAPTER SEVEN

**"Wherever you are, you aren't stuck--
You are a human being. not a tree!"**
Andrew Matthews - *Follow Your Heart*
-

Workshop #2

Lucinda and Brooksie drove into the visitor's parking area of the prison. "I've got to admit I'm still nervous about this place and having an inmate murdered around the time of our first workshop hasn't boosted my confidence level one iota," shared Brooksie. "I know Sharon hated to call and let us know what happened. I think she was afraid we wouldn't come back. I tried to reassure here that we are in for the long haul."

"Here we are ready or not." offered Lucinda. "I'm such a wimp, but I refuse to let Sharon see my cowardly side."

The two walked up to the admitting gate, arm in arm. The same check-in routine is followed and soon they were being greeted warmly by Sharon.

"So glad to see you again. You deserve hazardous duty pay, but your rewards are not going to come in the monetary way. Can you stay a bit longer today after the workshop? I need to go over a few things with you." asked Sharon.

Both facilitators nodded. The group of inmates entered noisily as before. Everyone sat down and Brooksie greeted them.

"Good morning ladies. Happy to see all ten of you have returned. Lucinda and I reread the information you were kind enough to share with us two weeks ago. We spoke with Sharon by phone she told us about the loss of Simone. I'm sorry for those who cared for her. We hope the perpetrator will soon be brought to justice. The three or us agreed the best topics for this workshop are self-worth, messages received from childhood and what makes a person unique or special. The feelings of self-worth or lack there of, are usually part of the root causes of destructive behaviors beginning in early childhood. Eventually it is vital to acknowledge personal responsibility, for one's actions. That ideally starts in the teenage years."

Lucinda added, "If any of you have other suggestions or other topics, we are glad to consider them."

No one spoke up. A few moved around in their chairs, some picked at their cuticles or chipped off polish and all looked silently at the speakers.

Brooksie began, "The messages you were bombarded with as a child make up part of your feelings of self-worth. Many of you need to put the words together and acknowledge what the messages were. At least what you thought they were. Next it is time to reject those harmful voices of the past.

"Kids get bullied, shamed, become depressed or angry, feel helpless, may feel guilty for their parents outrageous abusive behaviors. You might have thoughts that say, 'if I was smarter, prettier, taller, a girl, a boy or whatever maybe my mother/father or guardian would like me and take better care of me. It must be my fault they don't love me. It would have been better if I'd never been born. That's what my dad and mom say a lot. I must be responsible for their poverty, neglect, addictions, cruelty, abandonment. I am a stone around their neck.'

"Your parents or whoever was raising you were simply wrong.

"Each of you is unique and were born with intrinsic value. The attitude about our human experiences are what make or break us. When we were children, we learned about life and about ourselves through those who were supposed to care for us. If we were deprived of the physical and emotional needs, then it's no surprise we started to believe that we were an unlovable, throwaway, a burden and held no value.

"A few of you may have come to the conclusion; I may be different, black, white, red, or yellow, I may be missing some body parts, maybe I'm blind, deaf, too short, too tall, too fat, too skinny, and so on and so on. All of which makes me unique. I am different. I am one-of-a -kind and that makes me a valuable member of the human race. I have something to give back to the world. But, it is up to each one of us to develop our character and find our calling."

Lucinda asked the group, "Does any of what Brooksie is saying sound familiar to you? Please think about it for a minute or two. We want you to remember who was responsible for your care when you were a baby, toddler, a youngster and up until the age sixteen to eighteen. What makes you unique and what are your talents? We are all born with a potential to do either good or bad deeds. It is our choice. Each day we have the chance to make the same choice or a new choice.

"Anyone willing to share what you remember about the treatment and the message you received as a child?" How did you see yourself? What did you believe about yourself?"

The group stayed quiet for a while. Lucinda broke the silence, "I have a mother from hell. I tried to do anything and everything to make her happy, and to like me for the past thirty years. The message I got was loud and clear. I couldn't do anything right. I was doomed to be a failure at everything. Last year I made the choice not to see her anymore. I finally figured out that I couldn't change her feelings or behaviors, but I could change mine. I wish I'd had a nurturing, caring mother, but I didn't. So I grieved and moved on. My mother's rejection did not diminish me as a person of potential, but it definitely diminished her.

"Maybe one thing that makes me unique is my courage. I made a tough decision and stopped my relationship with my toxic mother. What I thought about myself became far more important than what my mother thought of me. I must add, I've had great friends who continually offered support and encouragement to me. They often remind me of my strengths. My mother only reminded me of my flaws."

Houston took the lead, "What makes me unique is my loyalty. I'm a protector of the underdog. I see myself as a warrior. The message I got from my dad was to stay out of his way. I don't believe he ever thought I was a cute baby. To him I was another unwanted mouth to feed. I was in the way and took up too much room. My mother wasn't present. She was practically invisible. I can't even remember what she looked like without a black and blue face. Her eyes were always swollen. I never heard her laugh. It was my grandmother who showed me love and kindness. She did the best she could to make up for my lousy parents. She had the softest blue eyes and smelled like a warm cookie."

"Do you think some of the harmful choices you've made as a grown-up have been influenced by the way you were parented as a child?" asked Lucinda.

"Can't say I've given it any thought. My dad was mean, drunk and sober. My mom was a coward and frightened of everything. Never been a drunk, I'm not mean and I'm not a coward. I can't blame them for the shit I've pulled. I don't know what you're getting at," questioned Houston.

"You're right about not blaming them for your adult bad choices. What is the message you received about yourself as a child growing up with a mean dad and an invisible mom? You mentioned you felt like you were a burden, in the way, another mouth to feed. Perhaps you began to feel damaged, unwanted and even in danger. You had a puppy who showed you only love and you could love it back. You couldn't protect your sweet puppy from a mean dad and your mother never tried to save the puppy or you. Now you protect those who are unable to protect themselves, a good choice. Is it possible the false message from your parents planted itself deep inside you? You bought into it and didn't really believe you deserved anything really good? Like good-hearted friends, a decent, loving partner, a career to be proud of, after all you weren't even worth feeding, protecting, loving as a guiltless, adorable child so what could you expect as an adult?

"So your saying if I expect shit for myself then I'm never going to get a box of candy and roses?" reasoned Houston.

"Right on." answered Brooksie.

Delores encouraged Houston to think better of herself. "You're really a good person and deserve a good life. I never blame others for my actions. I'm honest. That sounds pretty crazy since I drove my boyfriend to the liquor store knowing he was planning to rob them. I've also been an addict. I don't deceive myself about my mistakes and failings. I know my faults and even with all of the bad choices I've made I'm still an optimist.

"My folks parented by the book and the Bible. They never argued, never raised their voices, we had to pray before every meal. Actually we prayed a lot, meal time, bed time, and all day on Sunday. We prayed for everybody, especially for those who didn't attend our same kind of church. Mom and dad were pretty much flawless. They didn't drink, drug, or smoke. They didn't overeat, had no desserts, except on special occasions and most Sundays.

"It must tear them up to see me in prison, a common criminal and addict." Delores sighed deeply and under her breath added "They deserved better."

Sasha remarked, "Your childhood sounds like a nightmare. You were raised by two tight-assed Bible thumpers. No wonder you went so wild. They were suffocating you and your brother."

"I don't know about that, but they did want us to be just like them, real good," answered Delores. "My older brother Rick, the first born, was perfect in my parents' eyes. His death changed everything."

"More like God-like," whispered Luella.

"The messages I got were right to the point. I was made for pleasure and my body would provide an income. What makes me special is sex," teased Sasha. "I love it and love making a living at it. I don't need any damn degree, don't have to pay back loans, I owe nobody nothing. I'm pretty much self-taught except for Ray who showed me a few tricks when I was thirteen years old. He always said I was special and could see how talented I was. I could teach him a few things now."

Lucinda asked, "What do you think will happen to you when you get older and men don't want to pay you for sex anymore?"

"I've got twenty more good years. Later I might find a rich old fool and let him take care of me or maybe I'll teach young girls my trade and let them support me."

"You were a child Sasha, and Ray was a criminal. You are worth a great deal more than just a sex object." concluded Lucinda.

Sasha shrugged her shoulders and said, "Bet I have made more in afternoon than you have in a week. So don't look down on me just 'cause you can walk out of this stinkin' place whenever you want and I can't."

"You may be queen of orgasms, but you're one friendless bitch in here," snapped Wilamina.

Several inmates nodded in agreement. Sharon reminded the group of the rule of civility and asked the women to continue with the assignment.

Jackie spoke, "I'm kind. I believe that makes me special and unique. I'm also gay and that makes me part of the minority, nothing special or unique."

"Haven't you known any kind people in your life?" asked Brooksie.

"My brother is kind. He is also a kiss-up to our parents. He is gay and they have been cruel to him ever since they found out, but they still pretend he is straight. They give him a huge allowance to 'stay in the closet,' he takes their money and lies about dating girls, when in fact he has many male partners. All of our relatives have turned their pampered, oiled, cosmetically altered faces away from me. I could tell you stories that would make you want to throw up. I can list a thousand ways my so-called family has humiliated me over the years and intimidated Kent."

"You have always been very kind to me Jackie. I appreciate your kindness." offered Delores.

Jackie looked down at the floor, brushed a stray hair from her forehead and whispered, "Thanks."

"Could you tell us what messages you gathered about yourself from your parents over the years?" asked Lucinda.

"That's easy. I was born a freak, a mistake, something to hide and a punishment for my perfect family, " exclaimed Jackie. She wiped her face with the sleeve of her shirt.

Brooksie hesitated before addressing Jackie then gently said, "I cannot imagine what you must've felt like as a little child growing up in that toxic, hateful and twisted environment. You are a courageous woman who has demonstrated a powerful will to overcome adversity. You are amazing in a good way."

"We have something in common Jackie. Our families hate us and want us to hate ourselves and looks like they have succeeded," bemoaned Corrina. The names they called us were different, but they meant the same thing. My family simply told me I'm going to hell because I'm not fit to be with God. They are ashamed of me and want nothing to do with me.

"I'm a survivor, that's my specialty. I'm also friendly and oh yes, I have an excellent memory." bragged Corrina. "I can remember names, places and events for years and years. I can remember every guy's name I slept with and that is one hell of a long list."

"How did you do in school?" asked Brooksie.

"I hated everything about school. I quit in the tenth grade. It was a power trip for the teachers and principal. Everyone always tries to make you feel guilty if you didn't do things their way. They all make me sick."

"I envy your fine memory Corrina. I have to work like a maniac to learn new things. My memory is so poor," divulged Brooksie. "I agree with you that you share some horrible childhood messages with Jackie. Now you both have the chance to make choices no longer based on the lies you were brainwashed with as a little kid."

"Well, I can't think of anything special about me," stated Berri. "If my grandpa was alive he would say I was a pretty good fisherman for a girl. I like fishing. It's quiet and staring into the water always made me feel safe and content. I'd like to go fishing again, someday, at a lake high in the mountains." Her gaze drifted to the one large window in the cafeteria. "I don't know nothing about these messages you're talking about. We was poor and schooling was hard. My maw worked hard. She always took up with some guy who hit her and took her money. She never hit me. I think she was always tired and sad. She cried a lot. Makes me sad to talk about her."

Lucinda responded, "Thanks Berri for sharing what you did. I'm glad you have some good memories of fishing with your grandpa. I like to fish too. My husband and I are going fishing soon, maybe you could give me some tips."

"I can try. It's been a long time since I fished." answered Berri.

Sammy blurted out, "I'm unique 'cause I can understand animals, dogs especially. They have the same feelings we do and they can talk. Most folks just don't understand what the dogs are saying. The only time I feel worthwhile is when I'm with the dogs or other animals.

"Guess I got the same kind of message as a few of the others here got, when I was a kid. My parents kicked me out of the house twenty years ago when I told them I was gay. It seems they were always mad at me. I'm not sure I even knew why they were so pissed off. They fought with each other all the time. My home was an arena. Maybe that is why I picked such a difficult partner. She liked to argue about everything. The only joy I had was with my dogs. My dad used to scream at me saying, 'You go live with the pigs.' I'd rather live with pigs than most people."

"You would get along great with my aunt. She talks to all kinds of animals and has made it her life's work to find homes for every stray or abused animal on the planet," informed Brooksie. "I have a wonderful menagerie gifted to me by my dear aunt."

Wilamina blurted out, "I don't know what this unique word means, but sounds like it's what can I do that others can't. I have a good voice. I use to sing my lungs out in church as a kid. I sang all the time no matter where I was. My granny was also complaining about my loud voice, but my voice seemed to calm my mama."

Brooksie joined in, "Wilamina I would love to hear you sing today at the end of the workshop. Would you be willing to do that?

"Sure thing Ms. Brooksie. Remember I warned you about my loud voice."

"This is a big room and it needs a loud singing voice. I also want to add that you saved your brother's life, You defended the underdog. You are also a helping kind of person. You tried to help your grandmother and your mother. This shows compassion, kindness and thoughtfulness. I'd say that makes you a special person."

"Willy, I hope you ain't gonna sing anything churchie, like about Jesus." remarked Charlotte.

"Youse just got to wait and see, missy " responded Wilamina.

"There's nothing unique about me, stupid yes, but not special," said Charlotte. "I made the same mistakes my mother did. I fell for a good-looking bum, worked two jobs while he sat on his big ass. His idea of going to work was to rob a liquor store and get himself shot dead. My dad didn't get himself killed, but he did take off and he never returned. Been better if he had been killed. Dead people don't cause problems or hurt your heart 'cause you're always waiting for them to come back."

Lucinda responded, "Charlotte you are not afraid of hard work and that makes you special. Not many people I know will work sixteen hours six days a week. You were trying hard to be a responsible person and take care of your brother even when you were a child yourself. Apparently you were determined to survive and keep your family going. That took guts, determination and work.

"I'm wondering what message you received as a child about yourself."

"Not really sure what you are asking. I did believe that life was hard and I would probably always have to work. I didn't expect much from anybody. Mom has worked herself sick and I guess I thought I would do the same."

"Here I am again the one out of place." stated Delores. "I had it easy and fouled it all up. I was a good nurse. I liked working the emergency room. It was challenging because there was something different taking place every day. You never knew what was going to come through the emergency doors. I've always liked a challenge.

"The message I got was simple. I could do anything I set my mind to. Challenges are what makes life interesting and exciting."

Brooksie responded, "Liking challenges definitely makes you unique. A great number of us homo sapiens will do much to avoid any kind of a challenge. So perhaps you can consider attempting to jump through hoops to get your RN license reinstated or if that is not possible, beginning a new career and starting over again."

Delores hesitated a moment and then said, "I'll give that challenge some serious thought Brooksie."

Lucinda looked over at Luella, "Luella, you are the last one to tell us what message you received from childhood and what's unique or special about you? What are you passionate about? What do you enjoy doing?"

"Dad did most everything. Mom tried, but she just wasn't very smart. I got the message I needed to grow up fast and help dad. I like to get dirty and sweaty working the dirt, planting, weeding or picking. I don't mind the heat and I love the smell of turned dirt. I'm not a bad person when I'm not all doped up. I'm just weak."

"Luella, apparently you have an appreciation and love of the land-earth connection. You appreciate the process of working the dirt, putting in the seeds, the importance of water and then the careful caring of the new growth. You also know how to be grateful for what your father has been doing for his family for many years." expressed Brooksie. "It seems as if our time is up and I want to make sure there is enough time left for a song from Wilamina."

Wilamina stood up, straightened her ill-fitting shirt and cleared her voice several times and began to sing *Amazing Grace.*

There wasn't another sound in the room except for Wilamina's clear and powerful voice. The music came from deep within her soul. Smothered sniffling could barely be heard, all eyes staring at the person with the special voice.

CHAPTER EIGHT

**"If you want friendship, you
must be a friend first."**
Andrew Matthews - *Making Friends*

Facilitator's lunch date.....

Friday rolls around again and the four friends meet as usual at Table Talk Cafe.

Rachael began, " Has Sharon told you about slipping us some pills and asking us to get them to the Fairway Lab in the next county?"

"No she hasn't. Do you want us to ask her about the pills when we see her on Wednesday?" asked Brooksie.

Anita responded, "I think she will say something to you if she has a private moment. Sharon whispered to me, there are ears listening everywhere. The lab results will be sent to Dr. Gibran's private office, per Sharon's request. Then the results are to be shared with the Warden. She'll will probably share the info with the detectives. I'm beginning to get an uneasy feeling regarding Sharon's safety. She looks concerned, but tries to reassure us all is okay."

"I wonder if the young woman who was murdered had anything to do with the pills in question. Was an autopsy performed on her?" asked Lucinda.

"I don't know," replied Rachael. "You two are scheduled for next week. Maybe you can get Sharon alone for a brief moment and ask about her suspicions. Just be careful no one hears what you are talking about. By the way, have either of you had any run-ins with the guard Rank? He really comes on to Anita and me. More to Anita 'cause she is obviously younger and much cuter."

"I am not that much younger, but maybe a little cuter," giggled Anita.

"No. I haven't had the pleasure of his attention, how about you Lucy?" questioned Brooksie.

"Neither have I. I did hear a few inmates talking about some male guard who's causing a problem. I didn't catch the name." answered Lucinda.

"We have learned they call the guards CO's. I try, when possible to call them by their first or last names. The prison environment is tough on employees as well as inmates. Calling someone by their first name shows some needed respect and identity recognition." Brooksie added, "It's tough on me too. So many broken spirits and messed up bodies. Marino grew jaded and I can see why. I don't want to lose my optimism like he did."

"Enough shop talk, let's get to some personal news. Brooksie, how is it going with you and Luke?" asked Rachael.

"Funny you should ask today. Tomorrow we will have our first real date without Drake. With his devilish grin, Luke informed me that his parents are keeping Drake overnight. Not only did I break out in a sweat, I even blushed when he told me about the overnight plans. It's not like I'm some school girl virgin, but I know once you sleep with someone, the relationship changes. I know it does for me. Marino was the only other serious boyfriend I've ever had."

"You mean he was the only guy you ever slept with?" asked Rachael.

"I'm going to take the fifth on that one, Rachael." answered Brooksie, shifting uneasily in her chair.

"Luke might turn out to be a lousy bed partner, then you won't have to think about continuing the relationship. You do know that you can learn a great deal about a guy from his love making, don't you?" asked Rachael.

"Rachael, Marino was a wonderful lover, but we weren't in sync with other issues important to me. I already know how Luke and I feel about most things I cherish, so if we are also fine in the bedroom then what?"

"So you are hung up on commitment?" asked Lucinda." Your love of kids, pets, your grief work and prison programs are well known. Don't you think it possible you can have it all and Luke too? Yes, some adjustments will need to be made, but so what?"

"How can a person be a good mom and work full time? My mom was kind and loving, but she worked full time and dated a great deal. I was left on my own much of the time. I needed more guidance. I don't need to have my own baby. I'd rather raise some child who really needed a home. I think adoption is a good choice. I want kids, pets, work, and Luke; but I don't want to neglect any of them." concluded Brooksie.

"You've bragged on Luke a great deal, right?" asked Rachael.

"Yes. I know he works full time and still does a great job of taking time with Drake. He seems relaxed about everything. I'm afraid I won't be as good as he is. He welcomes life each day with open arms. I greet each day with a to-do list and feel guilty and disappointed in myself if I don't finish everything on my list."

"I have one last question. How far down on your to-do list is sex? inquired Lucinda with a twinkle in both eyes.

"When I'm near Luke it's at the top of the list in big red letters flashing off and on. It's damn embarrassing," answered Brooksie. "I'm not sure if he is really that interested in me."

Anita chuckled and the other two looked at each other and nodded.

"Time to hear about you Rachael and you Anita," said Brooksie, as she wiped her forehead with her sleeve.

"My classes are all going well. I'll be glad to finally finish and start working full time. But I must admit, I like the campus environment. I can see myself years from now, as a professor at some prestigious university." expressed Anita.

"Any romantic interests Anita?" asked Lucinda.

Anita coughed, took a sip of water and said, "I've met a nice man. His name is Chad. We've gone out a few times, to lunch, to a movie and once on a picnic. We can talk for hours and never run out of things to say. I haven't told my aunt about him yet. She still hates all males. I don't want to listen to hours of male bashing. It's like an obsession with her."

"How often do you visit her?" asked Lucinda.

"Not as often as I should. She was so good to me, but I can't be open with her. I feel guilty when I see her and guilty when I don't. I know what you guys are going to say, that guilt is a waste of time. I know that, but my feelings just refuse to cooperate."

The friends continued their personal sharings and eventually returned to their perspective cars and on to their jobs.

CHAPTER NINE

**"Most people would succeed
in small things, if they
were not troubled with great ambitions."**
Henry Wadsworth Longfellow, Drift-Wood

"Thanks for meeting with me this early, Malina. I understand you are as busy as I am. We are definitely both overworked and underpaid. I need to clear something up with you concerning Dr. Primm's trial programs. Even though you and I disagree on their value, nevertheless they are going to continue and be completed in the next five months. Most of the inmates participating in the program seem to be motivated towards setting personal goals. They have passed on their enthusiasm to other inmates who are now asking to be enrolled in the programs next time.

"My personal goals for these workshops are to improve the lives of the inmates in prison and out of prison. I would eventually like to extend the workshops to other prisons. Whenever the inmates leave, I want them to leave our environment better prepared to make it on the outside without resorting to any criminal activities ever again.

"I've never been exactly sure what your objections to the workshops are. Please share your concerns."

"Gladly," responded the assistant. "I also want a better future for each inmate. I'd like Lancers to become a model for other prisons. But I believe that Sharon, a convicted murderer, is filling the womens' messed up heads with impossible ideas and goals. Our budget is already tight. It will cost us money to hire the extra guard for the workshop days. I've been receiving complaints from many of the inmates not attending the so-called workshops concerning the special treatment being given to the few participants."

"Hold it right there Malina. Exactly what special treatment are the twenty participants receiving?" questioned Warden James.

"One good example is that Sharon is permitted to make extra phone calls to the four facilitators whenever she wants to, " stated Malina.

"Who told you this? asked the Warden.

"Several of the girls. Delores is one, I know for sure. She's in Miss Everett's group." I can't remember all of their names at this moment."

"I don't understand how Delores could possibly have known how and when Dr. Primm makes calls except the one call permitted to all inmates during the day in the hallway. Sharon has been permitted one extra call a week to the facilitators requesting supplies and getting suggestions for the workshops. She makes this call in my office when I'm present. Now please explain to me how Delores would have any knowledge of this so-called extra call?"

"Making an extra call per week in the privacy of your office sounds like special treatment, Florence," proclaimed the assistant with a smirk.

"Mrs. Smithers, you have not answered my question. Let me repeat it. How would Delores know anything that goes on in my office? You've had a bug up your behind concerning Dr.

Primm since she arrived. Perhaps you are overly sensitive to people with professional degrees. You are an intelligent woman but you didn't have the same opportunities that I or others have had for higher education. Because you came up the hard way, it does not diminish your capabilities in any way. In fact, you are to be applauded for your determination to advance in your field of choice. You overcame obstacles. My life has been so much easier than yours."

"This isn't about degrees hanging on the wall. It's about discipline. You seem to forget, Warden, that these women are criminals sent by the courts to pay for what they did. This is about consequences for their actions. You want to coddle and rehabilitate the masses. I thought our first goal is to keep the public safe from the bad guys. Our second goal is to improve the inmates' future."

The Warden took a deep breath to calm herself and then stated, "You still did not answer the question about Delores. That concerns me. For the record, my philosophy and goals differed greatly from yours. You apparently see no hope for the inmates' futures. And your goals have strictly to do with punishment.

"You are right that all these women had their day in court and were all found guilty. Many are chronic offenders. If we opened the gates and let them all out today, tomorrow most would reoffend and soon return to prison. I want them to be better prepared to make it on the outside so they won't keep coming back.

"I know how discouraging the recidivism rate is and that is exactly the purpose of Sharon's programs. The purpose is to cut the rate of recidivism way down! The programs are intended to send the women out with better skills and self-respect. If they can realize that with hard work and making changes they need not break laws to survive outside of these walls."

"I hope you're right. But my experiences and conclusions differ from yours. I'm unable to conjure up a rosy picture of the inmates' future behaviors. I think I'm more of a realist than you are. I guess time will be the judge," cautioned Malina.

"I would like more clarification as to the alleged multiple complaints from some inmates as to special treatment given to the twenty participants and Dr. Primm," reiterated Warden James.

"I could give you a few names, but I have an appointment with two cooks and some disgruntled guards. Could we meet again later?" asked Malina.

"Certainly," affirmed the warden. "Do keep me informed of all complaints. I appreciate all your help putting out the frequent fires. But I still need to know about specific problems with staff and inmates."

Malina responded while walking out the door, "Will do Warden. Later."

After the assistant exited and shut the door behind her, the Warden unlocked her desk and removed a small notebook. She proceeded to jot down some quick notes and then placed the journal back in the drawer, locked it and checked to make sure it was secure. When satisfied the drawer was locked up tight she placed the key back on the chain around her neck.

Sharon accompanied by Rank Johnson, the CO, as they walked down the hallway towards the Warden's office. Malina stopped in front of her and said, "Is everything okay, Sharon? Are you on your way to the see the Warden?"

"Yes, Mrs. Smithers, everything is going well. Have you received any feedback from the group participants yet?"

"Not really. Maybe it's too soon to see any result from the self-respect workshops. Respect may be highly overrated anyway. Consequences of one's actions are the issue. The inmates are not here because they don't like themselves, they're here because they are criminals. I don't mean to discourage you. I'm a practical kind of person. No rose-colored glasses for me."

Sharon hesitated a moment and then said, "You are correct about the criminal status, but it can be most difficult to like yourself if your childhood taught you to believe you are nothing but a mistake. Something not even a someone to be belittled, beaten, raped, thrown away, or just plain ignored. There is a rumor among the inmates that you didn't even have a 'Leave to Beaver' kind of upbringing.

Mrs. Smither's face turned beet red and she took a step back and placed herself directly in front of Sharon. "You'd better start looking over your shoulder Sharon. That too is a rumor that I heard." Malina turned around abruptly then left with her heels clicking loudly on the floor.

Sharon thinking to herself, *that woman reminds me of the wicked witch in the Wizard of Oz. The prison environment can certainly bring out the worst in some. I wonder how many are sent to prison simply as law breakers and leave as hard knocked criminals. How about the employees? What does this sort of place do to them? Maybe a workshop for the workers would help. I'll do some thinking about that.*

The CO knocked on the Warden's door. "Come in, answered Warden James. Thank you Rank. I'll notify the clerk when Sharon is ready to go back to her division."

"Okay Warden, but I can wait outside your office if you want and take her back myself." responded the CO.

"Thanks for your offer, but that won't be necessary."

Rank backed out of the office and closed the door.

"I don't like that man." said Sharon. "He's made lewd insinuations to a number of the ladies, especially the younger ones. Some of them have shared with me that he intimidates them and makes them very uncomfortable."

Warden James asked, "Are you aware of any actual advances he's made?"

"Houston told me he had been propositioning Simone. I never heard that from Simone, but I do believe Houston. I need to call Rachael today. I have to confess, I'm here to obtain the lab results of pills that were smuggled out and sent to a lab. Sorry I didn't clue you in before now. The results were to be sent to Dr. Gibran."

The Warden handed the phone to Sharon and then sat herself down and started looking over the huge stack of papers on her desk.

"Hello Rachael, any news?" asked Sharon. A short period of silence followed as she listened to the response. "Thanks Rachael, see you Wednesday. I really appreciate what you have done." Sharon turned her attention to the Warden. "Rachael spoke with Dr. Gibran. Dr. Gibran said she has the results, but needs to give them to you first. I feel like a kid who got their hand caught in the cookie jar. Again, I apologize again for going behind your back. But I've heard several complaints of poor treatment of multiple ailments. I've been documenting names, dates and other information. I believe drugs are being sold to inmates and possibly others by Dr. Ronan and maybe his nurse, Janet."

"Do you know how serious your accusations are? I'm sorry to say that you're not exactly a credible witness, because you do have a criminal record. We are going to need real proof. Rest assured Sharon, I'm taking this information very seriously and will definitely follow up on other leads. Please watch your back and carefully choose who you share your suspicions with. This needs to stay between us for the most part, at least for now."

"Funny you should use the same words that Mrs. Smithers just said to me a few minutes ago about watching my back." stated Sharon. "To answer your question, yes, I know how serious my accusations are I will add that I believe they are only the tip of the iceberg."

Later on the Warden was alone in her office and she thought to herself, *what the hell is going on. What have I been missing? Dr. Ronan seems efficient and personable. I've got to pay more attention to Malina's observations. She is definitely street smart and has great instincts.* Pacing around her desk for a few minutes she decided to place a call to Dr. Gibran's home.

"Hello this is Dr. Gibran speaking."

"Dr. James here. Sorry to bother you at home, but by any chance have you received the autopsy report on Simone and the lab results of the pills sent to an outside lab?"

"As far as the autopsy report on Simone, I don't have it in front of me. But, I did see the copy that Dr. Ronan had on his desk. I can tell you what I read. The dead woman had zero drugs reported in the Toxicology report. I did get the report of the pills that were sent to a different lab. The pills were sugar pills, so called placeboes."

The Warden took a deep breath and said, "That lab report only confirms what the police department has been aware of for months. I'm embarrassed to say how ignorant I've been. Please share with me what you read about the autopsy."

"It said there were no drugs found in her system. There was bruising and an imprint of fingers on her throat, blood found on her teeth, not belonging to the victim. She had a torn upper lip. Blow to the back of the head eventually was cause of death. Won't you be getting a copy from the police department?" asked Dr. Gibran.

"Yes I should. I will call Detective Yomoto if I don't receive a copy today. Thanks Dr. Gibran and again I apologize for interrupting you at home."

"Actually I'm glad you called. I've been wanting to set up an appointment with you to discuss some concerns. Could I come tomorrow around 4 p.m.? That would give me one hour with you before I start my shift."

"I've got you down on my calendar for tomorrow at 4. See you then." The Warden slowly puts the phone down and thinks to herself, *This has been one wild week. Feels like some difficult days lie ahead. I must do better if I want to continue as the warden.*

CHAPTER TEN

"We do not have to live out our circumstances."
Rita Pierson TED video

Workshop #3

The group gathered again with noisy chatter and jabbing taunts from Sasha to Wilamina.

"Ladies please take a seat and let's get started. How does it make you feel when I address you as ladies?"

"Makes me wonder who the hell are you talking to?" snickered Sasha.

"Makes me sit up straighter," responded Berri.

"Thanks ladies for your responses," said Brooksie. "If we are addressed as pig, stupid, hey you stinky, shorty, fatty and so on, we may react differently both internally and outwardly. As a child, if we were constantly called demeaning names, we might grow up believing that we were worthless or damaged. If we heard belittling descriptions of ourselves throughout our youth we might believe we had no chance of ever amounting to anything worthwhile. Seems only reasonable we would want to strike out, because we apparently had no potential for a good life. Hope gone. That old saying that 'sticks and stones can break my bones, but names can never hurt me' isn't ever correct. When the ugly name calling goes on and on, especially by those who are suppose to love us, the name calling does hurt and may break us, at least for awhile.

"The themes for today's workshop are continued from our previous workshop. They are respect, choices, old messages and individual uniqueness. How can you get past all the ugly name calling from your childhood? One solution may be by simply admitting and recognizing that your parents, relatives, teachers, and others were wrong. You had no way of knowing because you were only a baby, toddler or a teen. They were actually talking about how they felt about themselves. They were cowards, liars and simply mean and selfish people. They were wrong! You had no way of knowing they were wrong because you were too young to understand."

Lucinda listed several words on the board in large print: Character followed by, kindness, compassion, tolerance, honor, integrity, responsibility and humor. These are the essential attributes necessary in building character. "If you will pay attention you will discover that you will have at least one opportunity everyday to treat yourself and possibly others in a kind way. Showing genuine concern for others you'll eventually find yourself being treated with more consideration." suggested Lucinda.

"The point being it's all about choice! You make the choice to either be kind to yourself and others or not. Choose. If you have honestly been looking at how you were treated as a child or young adult, you'd begin to understand that you were loveable, guiltless, precious being with potential for greatness. So I repeat, the adults were wrong when they called you a mistake or whatever cruelty hurled from their mouths. You deserved only affection and attention. Starting today, you make the choice of how you are going to treat yourself. You make the choice what treatment to expect and will accept from others.

"Sasha you are more than a sex machine. The man who taught you sexual tricks as a little girl, didn't care about you. He had a cash register for a heart. You were a child who was brainwashed and abused. You were fighting for survival. You won't find your self-worth between your legs. It is in your heart. Are you brave enough to choose respect for yourself?"

"Who the hell are you people to tell me how to live my life. Money is what is respected. People listen to the rich. Money talks loud and clear. It's the fucking rich who rule the world." blasted Sasha. Her pupils were wide open, a little drop of saliva slid down her chin and she hurried off for the restroom. Ms. White ran directly behind her.

"Jackie, you were raised by a nanny instead of your non-working mother. What message did you understand about yourself?" asked Lucinda.

"Guess I thought there was something missing in me. I wasn't a pretty, dainty, little girl. I hated the frilly dresses mom wanted me to wear. I didn't play with dolls and I soon realized my mother liked her friends' little girls better than me. She was always comparing me to Rachael and Lizzy. They were actually in beauty contests when they were six and seven years old. I believed I was an embarrassment to my mother and her fancy friends.

"Dad never crossed her. When I finally figured out I liked girls, not boys, except for my younger brother Kent, I was relieved. At the same time, I was terrified of the reaction of my parents, especially my religious mother's.

"I told them I was gay right after my high school graduation. They were appalled and told me to get out of the house and not come back. My mother disowned me. Dad said nothing. He just stared at his shoes. She also forbade me to see Kent. Her words were, 'I don't want you to turn him into a freak like you.' Darian, my older brother was in seminary at the time. He told me I was going to hell unless I changed, but he would pray for me. Change what? I never want to be like Darian or my parents.

"By then I felt fairly certain that Kent was also gay and hinted that to the three of them. My mother started to hyperventilate and threw herself at me. She was able to bloody my nose before I could free myself from her. Again, my dad did nothing, said nothing and never even looked at me. To this day, Kent never admitted his sexual orientation to our parents. He's not about to jeopardize his inheritance and all the financial support he gets every month.

"Mom gives him a hefty allowance. It's basically to keep him in the closet. That way she can remain in denial and save face. He is living two lives, one straight and the other gay. I can actually understand why he does what he does. I love him no matter what. He will always be my baby brother.

"Sorry about going on and on. I will say one more thing. Our nanny was my saving grace. She loved me and still does. If it hadn't been for her, I would have probably killed myself or my parents a long time ago."

Lucinda inhaled deeply then said, "Wow! What a lot of pain to swallow for a child and for so many years. I respect your strength for not committing some violent act. I don't know your parents, but they turn my stomach sour. Like Brooksie said, your parents were and still are wrong about you, since day one. Thank goodness for your nanny. So the question for you is; can you or will you choose to respect yourself enough to treat yourself with kindness and to recognize your personal self-worth?"

Jackie hesitated and then answered, "I can't imagine changing my opinion of myself overnight. Feels like giving up an addiction. I have tons of hate and bitterness for my family. Even my baby brother has never stuck up for me. He is too afraid of making mom mad. Guess I could stop smoking. That would be a step in respecting my body, wouldn't it?"

"That would be a great first step in showing care for yourself," answered Lucinda.

"I'm trying to think of something good about me," said Wilamina. "Can't think of anything."

"That's because there is nothing good about you." responded Corrina.

"Shut up Corrina," yelled Houston. "Nothing but shit comes out of your mouth all the time."

"Ladies, keep it civil or we will end this session right now and you will all be the looser's," responded Sharon.

"Yes ma'am," said a contrite Houston.

Brooksie addressed Wilamina, "You have treated Lucinda and myself with respect since our first meeting. I see you and Houston as defenders of the underdogs. That is an admirable trait."

"Guess you're right. I did defend my brother from my boyfriend. I did have to take care of my mama, grandma and Royal since I was thirteen years old. Mama wasn't right in the head after her boyfriend beat her almost to death. We was real poor. We got government checks to live on. Mama refused to give her boyfriend anymore of our welfare money, he got mad and beat her bad. I tried to stop him, but he was bigger than me, so I ran to the neighbor and she called the police. Julian went to jail and mama to the hospital. She was never the same. Grandma was old and crippled up with the joint aches. Julian always told me I was good for only one thing, guess I believed him."

Lucinda looked around the group, her eyes settled on Charlotte who was fixated on her hands, slumped down in her chair. "Charlotte, do you think you were treated respectfully as a little girl?"

"I don't know ma'am. Ma was always working. After my baby sis died, dad left us and ma had to work even more. My brother and I took care of each other. He was six and I was seven. Ma was trying to keep us fed and dressed. There was no time for respect, only time for work. There's nothing respectful about being dirt poor."

"There's nothing to be ashamed about it either. You were a child. Not your fault about the hard times." added Houston.

"Did you and your brother go to school?' inquired Lucinda.

"Some lady came to our house and told ma she would have to send us to school or we would be taken away to live with foster folks. Ma got a neighbor to drop us off at school and she'd pick us up after work. Raynard and me both liked school, we got lunch and the teachers helped us with learning.

"I left school in my last year to marry Jackson. My brother graduated the next year. I'm real proud of him. He did right. I did wrong. Ma is sick now and Raynard looks after her. Wish I could help."

"Sorry about your mother. Maybe you could send her a note asking how she is doing. Do you know you can take high school courses while you're here and even graduate? asked Brooksie.

"Yes. I just don't see any reason to. Simone was gonna to take classes with me, but now she's gone. Maybe she is better off. I sure liked her."

"Would you be willing to talk to Sharon about some classes?" asked Brooksie.

"I guess so."

Sharon spoke up, "Charlotte see me today after lunch. I've got some ideas I'd like to share with you."

"Sure thing doc and thanks."

"I hope you'll like school better than I did Char," stated Corrina.

"I take it that school wasn't your finest memory Corrina?" asked Brooksie.

"You've got that right. They give you tons of busy work that has nothing to do with nothing. The teachers are hypocrites. They want you to think they're smarter and better than you. The nuns were the worst. They only talked to me about hell and I was headed straight for it. Hell, I was only thirteen and hadn't done anything bad up to that point. They told me they knew I was thinking about bad stuff all the time and that was enough to send me right to the devil.

"I was stupid, but I loved Jose and wanted him to love me back. He kept asking me to prove how much I loved him so finally I did and nine months later I had a beautiful baby. I was sixteen years old, pregnant and Jose married me. We had a church wedding, I wasn't showing yet, but everyone knew about the baby. His family and mine all said I had tricked Jose. It was Jose who was the trickster. My baby died soon after being born. My grandmother told me it was punishment for giving my virginity away before marriage. The Catholic priest married us and the same priest signed our divorce papers. He called it an annulment. Even the church lied to me.

"Since I was already hell-bound I kept trying to have another baby by anyone who'd have sex with me. I didn't want no damn wedding or husband, just my own baby to love and who would love me back. Yes I was stealing and dealing drugs, but I stayed clean and sober hoping to get pregnant."

Brooksie wiped away several escaping tears and said, "I'm angry way down deep inside at the injustices you have been exposed to. Your family, priest, nuns, teachers, Jose and his family were all wrong. You were a young, innocent, hopeful, loving young girl. You were deceived by all of the adults in your young life, including Jose. They also tried to steal your future by distorting your belief in yourself. I'm truly sorry about the death of your most wanted baby. It might be helpful for you to obtain the hospital records of the birth and reasons for the death of your baby. Something to think about.

"I'm thinking of many nasty words to describe the hurtful, hateful adults in your past, but you alone need to name the crimes against you and then set them aside, decide how you want your life to be from this day forward. . Here comes that word again, choice. You are the only one who can choose a better today and tomorrow. What would that look like? What tiny act could you do today to show you understand those people from your past were all wrong? What positive behavior could you begin today?"

"I don't have a clue." responded Corrina.

"Sign up for a class. Something you're interested in 'cause you've got a good mind and a great memory. I'll sign up if you will. I'm for sure going to need help. You could be like a teacher for me. What do you say?" asked Charlotte.

"I'm not sure I can be much of a teacher, but why not try. Okay Char, your on."

"I'm ready to take my turn," said Sammy. "The message I understood was loud and clear. I wasn't the kind of kid my parents wanted. I was wired differently from them. I was a tomboy from the start. I liked playing sports with the boys. I liked being with the guys and felt out of place with the girls. My dad liked to have me hang along when he went fishing or fiddled with his car. My mom yelled constantly at both of us. She was always irritated with everything I said or did. She didn't respect nothing or anyone. She was boss and didn't give a damn about dad or me.

"I always loved animals, mostly dogs, big dogs especially. Thought I wanted to be a veterinarian, but my grades were poor. I couldn't learn from some teachers. I just couldn't get what they was asking of me. I didn't fit in so I had to settle on just working for a vet. I loved my job working for Dr. Blackmore. He said I was a natural healer."

"You've got something in common with Brooksie. She is an animal lover and advocate, too. I understand your vet and a few animal advocates visit you on a regular basis. So they must definitely see you as a worthwhile person," said Lucinda.

"Yeah, guess I'm not a complete waste."

"Another case of someone's parents being wrong," added Brooksie. "Perhaps you would be willing to help us start a program of inmates training rescue dogs?"

"In a heartbeat. Just let me know what I can do. I bet my vet would also be interested in helping out also."

"Sammy, that sounds like a great match for a program with dogs and inmates," offered Delores. "My parents taught me I was a great kid and could do anything I set my mind to. So you are right Brooksie, my parents were wrong. I ignored their support and loving message and threw my life away. Shame on me." contended Delores.

Lucinda responded, "You are only thirty-two years old. You could possibly live another seventy years! You have plenty of time to remember the message your folks brought you up with. You have time to show them they didn't waste their breath. You could prove them right by starting today! You can begin acting like a great kid that can do anything she sets her mind to.

"I assume your RN license has been revoked, but isn't there a possibility after a certain number of years of proven sobriety you could reapply? I don't know about the felony charges and licensing, but you could begin a search on the legal issues of reinstatement. That is if you are interested." asked Brooksie.

"I never thought about that, I just assumed my nursing days were finished. Guess I could check it out. One of the nurses in the infirmary could probably help me find out."

"Sounds like a good plan Delores. Please keep us informed about any progress." requested Brooksie.

Berri spoke up in a quiet voice, "I don't understand this message stuff. Some days there was food and I ate good, some days not so good. Sometimes I got hit 'cause I done bad and more times I got hit for no reason. If they was in a good mood, okay, but if they was in a bad one, look out. I never thought about tomorrow. I loved my babies. They was pure love. I could just hold them while they was asleep and it made me feel good."

Lucinda looked at Berri with tenderness oozing from her eyes and said, "You were pure love when you were a baby. Maybe if you had been treated the same way you treated Ali you would have felt better about yourself. Most everyone has hopes and dreams for a loving future.

"You and Corrina both have had babies you wanted and loved, die. Grief is a powerful emotion. The death of a beloved baby is life changing. It doesn't have to be a change for the worse, at least forever. It can bring forth something good. You have both stated you're overweight and have high blood pressure. Perhaps you can become a support group of two and encourage each other to choose healthy foods and exercise. Maybe you will think about it," suggested Lucinda.

"Maybe I could lose some fat too?" Charlotte asked in a hopeful way. "My mom had to work two jobs, 'cause pop walked out. He actually he snuck out and never came back. She tried hard to give my brother and me I what we needed. I felt sorry for her and guilty 'cause she had two kids to take care of. She was always tired and never smiled or laughed.

"I wound up with a bum and worked two jobs, just like my mom. She is sick now. I know she is disappointed that I'm in prison. My boyfriend, Jackson, was good looking like my dad and a lazy bum. I was thrilled he wanted me. What an idiot I was and probably still am."

"Do you or did you ever daydream about seeing new places or having a certain kind of job or living in a special place of your own? How would your friends and family treat you in your fantasy world?" asked Brooksie.

"I did daydream a long time ago." answered Charlotte. "I thought I would like to have a small cafe and a few acres to raise chickens and maybe a horse. I'd plant a vegetable garden like my mom had. My brother and I helped to take care of it. I liked having my hands in the garden dirt. Clean dirt smells great."

Luella spoke up, "My pop worked in the fields. He knew all about growing grapes and tomatoes, garlic and peppers. He is real smart." Luella looked from one facilitator to the other with her head held high while she talked about her dad. "He taught my ma to pull weeds and how much to water the garden. He worked long hours under the hot sun. He cried when the foster people came to take away my two babies. I was a bad mom. I liked the drugs too much. I couldn't get myself together and ma had a bad brain, always did."

"Sounds like you admire your father because he is a hard worker and helped his family." remarked Lucinda.

"He is a good person. Ma did her best, but she always had trouble learning anything. She forgot all the time and had to be told over and over again. School was hard for me too. I gave up trying."

"Do you dream much, Luella? asked Brooksie.

"Not so much now. I use to when I was using. The doc said some drugs 'cause lots of really scary dreams."

"Can you remember any recent dreams?" inquired Brooksie.

"Sometimes I'm walking barefoot in the dirt. There are plants like beans and tomatoes and I feel happy."

"The next time you remember a dream please write it down and then share it with this group." said Brooksie.

"I will, if I dream again."

"I can take a turn at this," said Houston. "I don't remember anyone trying to make me feel bad about myself. My family life just was. Dad was a jerk. He never got past the third grade. Seems like he was jealous of mom. He was always accusing her of cheating. After he was sent to prison, she went sort of crazy. There were lots of guys coming and going in our shack of a house. A few sickos forced sex on me. Starting when I was around ten and continued till I was a teenager. I started going to bed with a knife. I actually used it a few times and cut on two assholes. Nobody bothered me much after that.

"My mom wasn't mean, she was just messed up. She ruined herself with booze, drugs and a shit-load of no good men. I felt sorry for her, she was empty inside. My brothers and me didn't see happy much. We only saw the violent and hopeless side of life. Two of my brothers mostly lived in the street. They ran with a real bad crowd. I never blamed them for leaving our house of hell. I did what I had to, to keep my shrinking family together.

"Guess what I'm saying is, the message I got as a kid was survive. Do whatever you have to to make it to the next day."

Brooksie hesitated for a moment, wiped her eyes then spoke, "Houston, you are an amazing woman. Your childhood sounds more like a war story. You battled other peoples' demons even when they turned on you. You were assaulted, emotionally and physically raped, abandoned and betrayed. Yet you still fought on. Your sense of responsibility, compassion, loyalty and courage leave me almost speechless. You have been surviving in a war zone your whole life. You deserve a Purple Heart plus all other medals that are usually reserved for war heroes. You are one of a kind, one of the best among us."

"I'm ashamed of myself for hating so hard and for so long. You kept your eye on survival of your family," said Corinna remorsefully.

"Houston, I'd I be proud to be your business partner when we get out of this joint," added Wilamina.

"Our time together is again over," announced Brooksie. "You all have much to think about for the next two weeks. Thanks again for your active participation. Perhaps you will choose to begin today by putting your goals into action, your choice. Looking forward to seeing you all next time."

Sharon signaled for the two facilitators to walk with her over to the corner. They followed Sharon and sat down on a bench next to each other. Sharon leaned in to them and whispered, "Please inform the Warden that there is a rumor going around that Loreli Woods has been going to the infirmary on a regular basis. We know how manipulative she can be. It might be worthwhile to investigate why she is visiting the infirmary so often. Thanks girls. The four of you are doing a great job. The program is looking promising so far. See you later."

CHAPTER ELEVEN

**"For, you see, each day I love you more.
Today more than yesterday and
less than tomorrow."**
Rosemonde Gerard, *"L'eternelle chanson"*

Date night......

Brooksie paced back and forth on her front porch waiting for Luke to arrive. She wore bright yellow pants, a blouse, tennis shoes and she had a fire engine red sweatshirt draped over her right arm.

Luke's almost new Suburban pulled up. He jumped out and said, "Hi there! Am I late or are you just eager to see me?" His full-faced smile accentuated his dimples and teasing eyes: seeing him, made Brooksie take quick short breaths.

"You're right on time. I just feel so guilty when my critters look at me with those sad eyes when they realize they are not going on an outing with me. I stepped outside so I won't have to look at their pleading faces. Am I dressed appropriately?"

"You look great! And I love your choice in colors!," added Luke.

"I chose the brightest colors I could find in my closet. I figured if you decided to dump me in the woods someone would eventually spot the red and yellow and send for help." An almost noticeable smile cracked her lips."

"Actually, we are going to drive through some wooded areas and wind up at a very special restaurant. It is way out in the boonies. In the middle of a farm with goats, horses, hayrides and grapes," responded Luke.

"Sounds terrific. Let's get started."

Fifty minutes later, they arrive at Paradise Ranch. It was easily identified by a large iron sign hanging from the overhead structure. The sign was held up on both sides of the driveway entrance by two large vertical beams. A smaller sign on the post read. Two Miles Ahead. The road parallels a pasture where several horses and even more goats of all sizes and colors are grazing. A few young looking goats were jumping on and off various kinds of structures built obviously for their enjoyment.

"I love this place already. Goats are so entertaining and full of energy. They are so playful and jump from one thing to another for the pure joy of movement. Look over there Luke, two Alpacas. You've brought me to heaven. I'll bet you have brought your son here before."

"Yes I have many times," answered Luke. I've even dragged my citified parents here and they've fallen in love with this ranch and its owners. Maybe your Aunt Tilly and Uncle Joe would like to visit?"

"Are you kidding! They would never want to leave. How did you find this treasure?"

"My long time friend, Jack Williams and his parents own this fine establishment. He and I have been buddies for over twenty years. Growing up, we lived next door to each other. Speaking of trouble here he comes." Luke introduced Brooksie to Jack. She puts out her hand for a handshake, but Jack grabbed her into a bear hug. Surprised and slightly winded, Brooksie tells Jack how glad she is to meet him and how much she loves his ranch and menagerie. "This ranch is perfectly named Paradise." she adds.

"Honey, you must be some special gal for hard-to-catch Luke to bring you out here. Drake and the Johnsons are regular visitor here. But never a filly has he thought fit to visit our fine place."

"Jack, you still talk too much. How about pretending to be a host and find us a table, away from your prying eyes and nosey ears," requested Luke as he thumped his friend on the back.

"You got it buddy." Jack winked at Brooksie and took them to a beautiful outside patio overlooking a vineyard.

A delicious and beautifully prepared meal was brought to the table. The meal consisted of salmon, roasted potato, fresh salad, all ingredients grown on the property. Wine from the ranch's own grapes, was served. The meal was topped off by a slice of fresh peach pie. After dinner, Luke suggested they take a walk to the stables. They were joined by four other couples. All were treated to a picturesque hay ride. The ride took them on a tour of a portion of the ranch. It was a relaxing end to a wonderful meal.

"Time to head home," said Luke. "Do you think you'd like to come back here sometime?"

"Are you kidding. I could move here in a heartbeat. I feel so at peace here watching the goats play and the horses graze. The vineyards are beautiful. I swear I can hear the grapes growing in this peaceful setting. Thanks so much for this wonderful adventure."

"Before I take you home I'd like to show you where I live. Is that okay with you?" asked Luke. He never took his eyes off the road, but was aware of Brooksie stirring around in her seat. It tickled him that she was somewhat uncomfortable with his suggestion.

Brooksie inhaled deeply. She could feel moisture forming under her armpits and on her forehead. "That would be fine. I'd like to see where Drake calls home.

A little more than an half an hour later they pulled up to a wrought iron gate which opened when Luke pushed a button. They were facing a one story house with a wrap-around porch. The outside of the house was half stucco and half stone. There was a detached four car garage. Her eye looked towards the wide stoned pathway leading up to a impressively large, carved front door. The path was lined with a variety of beautiful flowers and foliage.

"This is so outstandingly beautiful. The path, the plants and your carved front door take my breath away. How long have you lived here?"asked Brooksie.

"About eight years. I designed it and worked with a contractor that let me be part of the crew. It took me longer to finish the garden than it did to build the house. I Just finished the yard a couple of years ago. I have ten acres, altogether. Most of it is still in a natural state. My landscaping business has grown so quickly that I don't have much time left over to do anymore with the property. I have thought about adding a plant nursery. Still thinking about it.

They walk inside his home. He walks her from room to room. The patio in the backyard shows off a built in barbeque and a large stone fire pit. Large windows throughout the house admit great light during day hours. High ceilings and dark wood floors add a sense of strength and stability to the place.

"You have built a fine home, Luke. It is warm, friendly, classy and comfortable. You could have a career in designing or in architecture."

"I had help from my mother and a few of her cronies. They were afraid I would turn it into some Neanderthal cave. I inherited my sort of style from mom and my love of growing things from dad."

After the tour, Luke poured a glass of wine for the two of them and they returned to the patio as he directed her to sit beside him on the love seat. Once seated, Luke took her glass from her and placed both glasses on the table in front of them. He place one arm around her and with one hand he turned her face towards him. She offered no resistance. The kiss began gently, soon became intense and their breathing louder. Luke gently pulled away and handed the glass back to Brooksie. He then took a swallow from his glass. Music drifted outside from the kitchen. He asked if she would like to dance.

"I love to dance," she answered. They danced slowly for a time. *I can feel the beating of his heart. Oh God maybe that's my heart I'm feeling.* After a short time and the glasses are empty, Luke said, " It is getting late. Would you like me to take you home now?"

Brooksie wanted to yell out, "*Hell no*", but wasn't sure if Luke wanted to end the evening or not. *I know it would be better if we stop now. My body says stay, but my heart says, don't be a fool. Maybe he doesn't want me to stay.* "Yes I guess it is late and time to say thank you for a wonderful time."

On the drive back to Brooksie's house, Luke carries the conversation asking questions about her workshops at the prison. Brooksie gives a brief summary of the prison program, but she is distracted by her own confusion over Luke's exciting kiss and then the suggestion to take her home. *Maybe he's not interested in me. Maybe he just wanted the job. Maybe I'm a damn blind fool.*

Luke stops the car in her driveway and gets out, opens her car door and walks her to the porch. Booksie thanks him again and turns to put the key in the door. Luke turns her around and kisses her passionately until Brooksie starts to feel dizzy and frees herself.

"Would you go to dinner and dancing with me next Saturday night?" asked Luke.

"Yes. I'd like to do that. And thanks again for the great time today. Paradise Ranch is an unforgettable place." responded Brooksie.

Late into the night, Brooksie lies awake confused about Luke's behavior. *I don't understand him. I don't know if I should get involved or not. Cripes I don't even know if he's is attracted to me. I need a mentor or maybe a therapist. What I really need is a crystal ball. I'm such a weenie. I hate the unknown.*

CHAPTER TWELVE

"Patience is bitter, but it's fruit is sweet."
Jean Jacques Rousseau, Emile

Visiting day at the prison........

"Hi Mr. Blackmore. Sure glad to see you. How's everybody doing at your hospital?" asked Sammy. She moved quickly across the visiting area and grabbed the veterinarian's hand and shook it with enthusiasm.

"Good to see you too, Sammy. All the animal patients and staff are doing well. Mary said to say hello to you and sent along some hand lotion and candy. I do believe you've lost some weight and your hair looks different."

"Yes sir, I'm eating better and half-heartedly doing some silly exercises. I'm in a six month program that's supposed to make me a better person. Lucinda, one of the teachers has been giving me some tips about my hair."

"Aren't you coming up for a parole hearing soon?" asked Dr. Blackmore.

"I'm really not sure when. Maybe in about another five or six months." she answered.

"Sammy, if it goes well for you at the hearing I want you to know you have a job waiting for you with me, if that's what you want."

Sammy stared momentarily at the floor and puts a hand up to her face too late to catch the tears that started down her cheeks. "Are you sure you want me. What would your staff think?" Her voice shaking and she was losing the attempt to hold back the flow and keep control of her emotions.

"I can't tell you how much your kind offer means to me. All my life I've wanted to work with animals and now even after I've done a terrible thing, you are willing to give me back my job? You are a good man, Mr. Blackmore." She takes hold of both of his hands and squeezes.

"Would you like me to bring you a few books about the work of a vet assistant?" asked Dr. Blackmore.

"You bet! and I'll study'm day and night. I'll never know how to thank you," said Sammy tearing up again.

"Sammy, you have a special touch with animals, I will be the one thanking you someday. I'll bring the books by on my next visit. Bye for now and take care."

She watched him leave the area. As she slowly walked back to the common area, she continued to shake her head in disbelief for his unwarranted and kind offer. *There are some good people in this world, not just good dogs. I'm being given a chance to do something worthwhile, hope I don't screw it up.*

Sasha had a visitor. He was a seedy looking guy about forty years old. He had dark circles under his eyes, sallow complexion, extremely thin and dyed black hair. He constantly looked around the room. Their visit lasted only about fifteen minutes. Sasha wrote something on a small piece of paper, then handed it to her visitor. He placed it in his pocket and quickly stood up and started for the door. The CO manning the door asked to see the note. Mr. Wu Jones handed it over. The CO read it, then shook his head in a questioning way and gave it back. The visitor signed out and left.

Corrina had been waiting in the hall and was called to the visiting area. The CO Rank Johnson said to her, "You have a visitor, surprise surprise."Giving her a wink.

Corrina entered the area and quickly spotted her friend Maria. They embraced and sat down.

There is always a CO situated at the front desk near the door and several other CO's observing the visiting area on a catwalk above the room.

Maria handed her a small notebook and Corrina proceeded to hurriedly write something in it. She handed the notebook back to Maria. Animated conversation followed. Corrina's frown deeply wrinkled her forehead. She used her hands to talk as much as her lips. Maria dabbed at her eyes several times. The cheap mascara got away from her and left dark lines sliding down her cheeks.

Two of the observing guards, on the catwalk were talking to each other, "What do you think is going on with Corrina and her visitor?"

"Not sure, but I'm going to ring up Sparky at the desk and let her know she might want to take a look at the visitor's notebook." He called the desk and Sparky looked up and nodded to the guard holding a phone.

Delores was notified that her parents were waiting in the visiting room. She spoke to the guard as she entered the doorway, "I hate to see them because they cry every time." The three hugged and after the mother wiped dry her eyes dry, and took her daughter's hand and started into praying out loud. Delores eyes darted around the room to see who was listening to her mother's prayer. Delores inquired about her brother, in an attempt to distract her mother from her constant praying. "I do appreciate you making this long trip to see me, but I worry about your safety on the road. Please don't feel you need to come every month. I feel awful causing you problems and expense."

Just before her parents were ready to leave they held hands, closed their eyes and quietly say some prayers. They embraced again and the parents tearfully said their good-byes. Dee remained dry-eyed throughout the visit.

"Visiting time is over," announced Sparky. When Maria got close to the desk, she was asked to hand over the notebook for a look-see. Maria hesitated momentarily then handed it to the guard. The guard looked inside and silently read: underpants extra-large size, cigarettes, two candy bars, stationery with envelops and stamps and the last items were for books about self-defense and one titled 'If Grace is True.' The guard told Maria that she could only deposit money into her friend's account. The inmate can purchase items at the hospital store. Maria said she would do that today. She was directed to the business office. The notebook was handed back to Maria and she went on her way.

Thursday.....................

Houston was notified her attorney had arrived. As she started to walk toward a special room, set aside for attorneys and their clients, she stopped for a moment and talked with Wilamina. "Willy you should try to talk with my attorney Roco Lagunta. He's good, fair and his fees are reasonable."

"His fee would have to be almost free, that's about what I could come up with. Maybe I could pay $20.00 a month for a long time. Probably the rest of my life. My brother tells me he's got a good job and that he's sober. Maybe he could help some. now. He visited me last month and looked clean. Would you talk to your lawyer for me today?"

"Sure Willy. I'll ask him if he would see you. Gotta go now, Mr. Lagunta is waiting."

Houston enters the visiting area, spots her lawyer and quickly walks over to where he's sitting. They shake hands and she sits across from him. "Ms. Houston, I've spent some time going over your records. It appears you've had quite a number of fist fights with boyfriends. In fact, the last encounter ended in the death of one of your mom's boyfriends.

"Your warden speaks highly of you and tells me you have kept your nose clean for the past four years. She also mentioned you look out for anyone who is getting picked on.

"Please tell me about yourself. Please start when you were a child and end when you got into it with your mother's friend, Mr. Adams."

Twenty minutes later, Houston had summed up her violent past. She recalled the multiple beatings her dad inflicted on her mother, his disappearance and eventual incarceration. She continued by telling him about the numerous boyfriends her mother brought to their home, the molestations by two of the mother's men friends starting when she was around nine. Later on when she was older, she had three different boyfriends who all routinely knocked her around until she retaliated with her own fists. The death of Wilfred Adams took place when she had gone to visit her mother and found Wilfred beating her mother. Houston's protective instinct for her family jumped in and in her attempt to stop him from killing her mother, she beat him so severely that he died that same day in the emergency room.

"I read the transcript and I must tell you I believe you got a bad deal. My goal, if you agree, is to get your guilty charge turned around. You don't belong in prison. You are not guilty of premeditated murder. You were defending your mother's life."

"Mr. Lagunta, I've got to be up front with you. I've got no money to pay you for helping me."

"You'll not own me one penny. You have spent too many years incarcerated for rightly defending your mother. This needs to be set right."

84

"I don't know what to say. I've never had anyone go to bat for me before. It feels strange. Like maybe there's a catch."

"No catch, only justice. I will get the ground work started and I will have more questions for you later. Do you have any questions for me?"

"I hope you won't think I'm too pushy, but I want to ask you to see a friend of mine. She is also an inmate. Her name is Wilamina. She's here for the same reason that I am. She defended her brother from her own boyfriend. He was out of control and kept on punching and kicking her brother even after he had passed out. She killed her own boyfriend accidentally. She just wanted him to stop the beating. Would you think me ungrateful if I asked you to talk with her?"

"Give me her full name and I'll have my office staff look into her records. You can tell her I'll get in touch with her later this month. Anything else?"

Houston was frantically wiping away a torrent of tears. She couldn't keep up with the flow so she just let them run down her cheeks, as if a dam had broken.

"I just don't know what to say, " hanging her head and timidly touching his arm.

The lawyer responded, "I'll see you again in two weeks. By then I'll have a few more questions. Bye for now and please tell your friend Wilamina, I'll get in touch with her."

CHAPTER THIRTEEN

"Character is what a man is in the dark."
Dwight L. Moody
quoted in William R. Moody's *D.L. Moody*

The revelation that her prison has been under investigation for possibly six months had Dr. James reeling. *I'm fighting the urge to resign. I won't do it because it might hurt the detective's work, but how blind have I been. It's hard for me not to share these recent developments with my dear husband. He's always been so supportive and interested in my career. He's going to sense something is bothering me. I hate keeping secrets from him, but I will. Eventually I'll be able to clue him in. I better watch my P's and Q's. The detectives asked me to act natural. In that case, I better keep my appointment with Dr. Ronan as planned earlier.*

A short time later.........
Warden James greeted Dr. Ronan at the door. "Thought we could have lunch together in my office, Mitchell. I know you might have a tight schedule, but I'm finding it important to meet with staff once in a while. I want to keep abreast of any progress as well as problems that may arise. I had the kitchen staff make us some sandwiches and coffee. It's far from gourmet, but definitely filling."

Dr. Ronan replied, "Looks good, and so do you by the way. Do you have a new hairdo?

"Same one. Same old me, Mitchell. You may already know about the conversation I had with your nurse Janet. The police have a warrant for two inmates whom you have treated. I assume Janet filled you in concerning the files taken from your office on these two women?" How well do you know your nurse?"

Dr. Ronan replied, "Janet's been with me for about three years. She's always been efficient and reliable. I consider her to be a capable RN who performs her duties well. She doesn't put up with any nonsense from the inmates and is pretty good at spotting a malinger. She may be a little overprotective of me. I'm must admit being quite surprised and confused by your request. What are the detectives looking for?"

"I'm also in the dark, Mitchell. They offered me little information except to say they were in the process of gathering evidence, hopefully leading to solving the murder of Simone. Detective Yomoto added they will soon be conducting a number of interviews with some of the staff and inmates. He mentioned something about complaints from previous inmates and a few from relatives of inmates still incarcerated here."

"What sort of complaints are they referring to? Do they have any suspects?"

"They didn't elaborate. If they did, they didn't share any names or anything else with me. I didn't feel it was something I should question them about. I got the impression we are to go about our regular duties and they will let us know more when they can," answered the Warden. "Can you think of anyone who might have had a grudge or motive to kill the inmate, Simone?

"Not even a guess, Florence. Inmates murder inmates. That's been going on for a long time in prisons around the country. Why is this one getting so much attention?"

"You know better than to ask me specifics. Confidentiality is sacred. Especially here in the prison. Do you think there could possibly be a connection between your nurse and complaints from inmates about receiving no prescribed pain killers?"

Dr. Ronan's voice climbed an octave, "No way! As I said before, Janet has my complete confidence. I'm very surprised you would even suggest she might be doing something illegal. I do understand you are under a lot of pressure at the moment. Perhaps you are simply grasping at straws. You'll have to excuse me, I have a backlog of patients waiting. I better be getting back to the infirmary. Glad to spend some time with you, we should do it more often. You're running a fine prison. Remember you are dealing with a society of criminals. They have had lots of practice twisting information to suit their needs and wants.

"You must be aware of the fact that many inmates will say just about anything to get their hands on drugs of all kinds. The majority of them are addicts or have been in the past. Personally I usually take their complaints with a grain of salt. I'm suspicious by nature. It's probably why I work well in this system. Addictions and lying go hand in hand with this population. If you want, I will keep a closer eye on Janet, but she has never given me any reason not to trust her." He quickly stood up and moved toward the door.

"Thanks Dr. Ronan. I'll let you get back to your clinic. I would appreciate you keeping your eyes open for anything that seems out of the ordinary. One more question. Were you ever in private practice?"

"No, not really. I did a short stint with a partner many years ago. Private practice for a young doctor is too expensive. You need wealthy parents if you are going to make a go of it." He winked and made a hasty retreat.

She yelled after him, "Thanks again for your time. I won't bother you more than necessary. Good day Doctor." *He definitely believes in the power of flattery and is mister smooth. He is good-looking, but in a slimy sort of way. It seems like he was mighty anxious to end our conversation.*

CHAPTER FOURTEEN

**"The significance of a man is
not in what he attains
but rather in what he longs to attain."**
Kahlil Gibran

Workshop #4

Brooksie began, "Good morning ladies. Lucinda is passing out paper and pencils for you to write answers to the questions pertaining your personal goals. First, what do you hope to accomplish while locked up? Second what are your goals upon your release? And last, what do you see yourself doing when free?

"I'll throw out a few examples of possible goals: finish high school, be trained for a job, write to kids and family, work on improving relationships, lose weight. Please start writing down your ideas now."

After five minutes Lucinda, asked for volunteers to share what they had written down or what ideas they might have.

"I can start 'cause my list is short." offered Wilamina. "I want to lose twenty lbs. and read a book. Maybe a book about detectives and violent crimes."

Lucinda asked, "How will you go about starting to lose weight?"

"I'll start with no more second helpings of potatoes and no more desserts," answered Willy. "I'm already hungry just thinkin' about eating less."

"Sounds like a practical and doable plan. What could you do when you are tempted to take that delicious looking piece of cake?" asked Lucinda.

A grin starts across Willy's face and she answers, "I can look at some of the other fatties in the line and hope that gives me the strength not to reach for the good stuff."

"What about the book? How will you find the kind you may be interested in?"

"There is someone working in the library here and I can ask for help. I also know Houston likes detective stories so I can ask her for help."

Houston spoke up. "Sure you can. In fact, I've just finished one. We can go to the library together and you can check out the book I'm turning back in."

"Thanks Houston," said Willy.

Lucinda addressed the others, "Anyone else willing to share?"

Delores responded, "One of my goals it to learn Spanish. So I'm going to ask a friend to send me money. Then I will purchase a beginner workbook from the prison's store or maybe find one in the library. I can call her this week and ask her to deposit into my account here. I also like to read biographies. So guess I'll make a trip to our friendly library today and check out a book or two."

"Learning a new language is a fine goal and quite a challenge. You've said you like challenges and starting with a beginner workbook is a good way to begin. You're also surrounded by several Spanish speaking inmates who I'm assuming would be willing to help you if needed."

"My goal is to lower my blood pressure so I need to lose weight. For two weeks I won't eat potatoes or bread and see if

I lose anything. I will eat more vegetables which I don't like so well," bemoaned Corrina.

"What do you think would be a reasonable weight loss for two weeks?" asked Brooksie.

"Maybe ten pounds. I don't really have any idea." She answered.

Delores offered her opinion, "Two or four pounds would be more like it."

"Delores may be closer to the truth. It's important to not set yourself up for failure and disappointment." stated Brooksie.

"The goal I'm going to set for myself is to sign up for a business course." shared Houston. "When I get out of here I want to be my own boss. I'm not sure what kind of business yet, but I want to learn about how to start one up. Like how to keep books, pay taxes and what licenses I will need."

"You have a good workable plan to reach a goal. You will eventually figure out what sort of business you want to go into. Do you know when the class begins, Houston?" asked Brooksie.

"I can find out in the library. They hang a list of all classes, dates and times on the door." responded Houston.

Sammy was sitting up straight as an arrow and displaying a big smile and several missing lower teeth. Her whole face lit up as she told the group her plans. "I'm going to be a veterinarian's assistant, Dr. Blackmore is going to send the Warden the books that I need to study. She will check them out to make sure there is no contraband hidden in the pages. He has already spoken with her about the books. They have been friends a long time. He wants me to work for him when I get out of this joint. I'm going to be the best damn assistant he will ever have. I'd work for free for him. He's the only person who has ever treated me good." Her lips started to quiver and she hastily looked down and started to mess with her paper slippers.

"That is great news Sammy", offered Sharon breaking her self-imposed silence.

Several other inmates offered her congratulations and wished her well with her studies.

Luella shared her love of working in fields and orchards. She especially enjoyed picking fruit, because there was shade and you could eat your fill of the fruit. "My dad use to talk about wanting to work in a nursery. I wouldn't mind doing that with him. We both like getting our hands in clean dirt."

Sammy suggested, "Maybe you could look at some plant books. You could get to know what plant grows where you and your dad live."

"Good idea," agreed Brooksie. "I have a friend who could probably suggest a book or two. Where will you and your dad be living when you finish up your time here?"

"Dad lives in the Yakima Valley. He's told me he wants me to stay with him. He's going to help me get my two youngsters back from the foster family. Yes ma'am I would like to look at any book or books your friend suggests, I'd also like take some parenting classes."

In a low voice, Charlotte made a few remarks how horrible Luella had been as a mother and Willy admonished her, "You don't need to kick her so hard. She's already down on herself, Char. None of us here are saints and that means you too."

Charlotte slipped down in her chair, looked sheepishly at Luella and said, "Sorry Lu. I feel like a piece of shit and I struck out at you. I just always wanted a baby to love and to have someone who would love me back. I worked sixteen hours a day, six days a week and my fucking husband sat on his skinny ass. He spent the money I earned on every drug he could find. What the hell was the matter with me?"

Jackie faced Char and said, "It wasn't you that was wrong, it was your stinkin' boyfriend. We have opposite goals, Char. You want to make your mother happy and I want to make my mother as miserable as she has made me all my life." She pounded her fists against her thighs and her eyes roamed around the room, not really focused on anything in particular. "Mrs. Slauson, my dear nanny, raised me and still believes in me. She writes to me consistently. Visits me when she can and tells me over and over that my resentment for my mother is like food for cancer. I can't seem to stop myself. I want my parents and brother to suffer. They are my cancer."

"Your friend, Mrs. Slauson, sounds like a wise woman," said Brooksie.

Lucinda asked Berri if she had a goal in mind, "Maybe I could eat less. The night doc told me my blood pressure was bad, too high. She told me if I would lose some weight it would help lower it. I get bad headaches a lot. So I could do what Willy says she is going to do, no desserts and no potatoes.

"My problem is that I don't give a damn about living. My son Ali was everything to me. My worst mistake ever was when I left Ali with Sam one time. Sam was always yelling at me to keep the baby quiet. I told him Ali is a baby and babies all cry. I had to go to work that day but I couldn't get my aunt to watch my son 'cause she was sick. I really needed my job. Sam worked on and off when he was sober. I hid his gin bottle before I left that day so he would stay sober and take care of Ali."

Berri stood up at this point and started to pace back and forth. "He hit my baby. He hit him so hard his brain swelled up. His ribs were busted, blood was coming from his nose and mouth. A neighbor took Ali to the hospital. He died there. They let me hold his little broken body for a long time. They finally carried him away covered by his bear blanket.

"When I got home Sam was stinkin' drunk. I had rat poison in the house, 'cause I saw a few rats a few times. Rats give me the creeps. I kept staring at Sam. I felt like my head was gonna explode. I decided to make Sam my Cajun stew. He really liked it. I mixed lots of poison in the stew. He ate it all. Then came the pain. He screamed and cried. I turned the radio up loud so no one could hear him. I told him about the poison and about my baby's broken body. I watched that man die in agony and then I called the police. End of story. I just want to be with my babies. That's my goal."

Everyone remained speechless for what seemed an eternity. Finally after blowing her nose, Lucinda spoke up, "I cannot imagine how you felt when you saw little Ali all broken and dead." Her voice broke. She took a few deep breaths then continued, "I can understand why you poisoned Sam. I'm glad he can no longer hurt anyone else. You were not to blame for Ali's death. Sam is to blame, only Sam. Yes, you made a poor decision to leave your son with him, but you are not responsible for Ali's death."

For a while, all that could be heard was noses being blown and stifled sobs. Berri unsteadily took her seat, shoulders slumped and head down. Sammy, who was sitting next to Berri, cautiously placed a hand on Berri's arm and softly said, "I'm sorry about Ali."

Brooksie wiped her face then looked at Berri with eyes still moist. "There are many women who are living with abusive partners who are placing themselves and their children at risk. If you had a chance to say something to these women, what would it be?"

"Throw the bastard out. Any guy who gets drunk or drugged is a nothing. Don't screw around with anyone mean, lazy or addicted. Take self-defense classes, buy a gun and let them know just one strike from their fist, means one bullet from you. I got nothing else to say." Berri's face was shining with perspiration as she took frequent drinks of water from her paper cup. Willy refilled Berri's cup from the plastic water pitcher on the table. She wiped her eyes and nose repeatedly.

Brooksie addressed Berri again, "Thank you for sharing the story of your precious son, Ali and his tragic and horrific death. The grief you must have felt and still feel is overwhelming. When you share it with others, it will eventually open the door for releasing the intensity of the emotions. I'm repeating what Lucinda said about the only one responsible for Ali's death was Sam. I cannot feel what you felt then nor can I feel what you're feeling right now. But, I can feel anger toward Sam. I can feel pain and compassion for Ali and you. My tears today are for your suffering. I'm so very sorry for you unbearable loss. Perhaps one day you will be willing and able to help others that are living the nightmare that you have been living. A choice that only you can make, Berri."

Lucinda stated, "Sasha you are the only one who hasn't had a chance to share with us."

"My goals are still the same. To make lots of money and live the easy life. Maybe I would have different ones if I had a kid that was beaten to death by some guy. I'm thinking about taking a business course they offer here. It would help me when I get out of this hell hole. Maybe I'll even have a legitimate business someday."

"A business course while you are here sounds practical and beneficial," added Lucinda.

"Our time is up for today," announced Brooksie. "I'm looking forward to two weeks from now to hear how you have all done. I hope you will encourage and root for one another. If you find you would rather pursue a different goal, go for it. This is your life, your choice. You know best what interests you. Have a great week. See you all later."

Sharon signaled Brooksie and Lucinda to follow her to a corner table for privacy. "I believe you know I gave some pills to Rachael to have them analyzed. The results have come back and our suspicious are confirmed. The pills are placebos. Dr. Ronan and Janet have been handing them out as pain pills to some of the inmates. I want the workshops to continue as if everything is okay The Warden, Dr. Gibran and Mela Washington are all aware of the placebos and are keeping their eyes open for anything out of the ordinary. That goes for you also. The detectives are keeping our Warden in the loop. They are looking into Maxine Ritter's role in Simone death."

"Are you in any danger, Sharon?" asked Lucinda. "We are all concerned about your safety."

"I'm careful and I talk to the Warden regularly. She said that one of the detectives plans to ask me some questions this week. The detectives have been interviewing many of the inmates this past week about the murder. There is definitely some extra tension in the air. See you in two weeks."

CHAPTER FIFTEEN

**"Fate makes our relatives,
choice makes our friends."**
Jacques Delille, *Malheur et pitie*

The facilitators lunch date.......

All four arrived practically at the same time in the parking lot of the Table Talk Cafe. They gathered for a group hug, entered the cafe and found a booth off in a corner. Rachael started the conversation, "I feel bad for the Warden. She verified the results of the testing of the pills Sharon slipped to Anita and myself. Now we know for sure someone in the infirmary is messing with the drugs. So now both Dr. Ronan and his nurse are suspects. The night and weekend shift people are also suspect. Sharon said Dr. James is really shaken and is blaming herself for doing a poor job as the Warden. She also said Dr. James Warden told her the detectives are working diligently to identify the person or persons who murdered Simone. It seems the police know about the medication and placebo problem."

"According to one of the inmates, Dr. Ronan and Janet have been working together for a long time. If they are guilty of messing with certain drugs, it doesn't seem very probable that only one would be involved illegally. We need to remember they are innocent until proven otherwise," suggested Brooksie.

Anita lowered her voice to a whisper, "Do you think Sharon is in any danger? She has no way to protect herself in there. We've got to get her out. Maybe she could be transferred to some other place?"

"She would never want to leave Lancer's at this point because of the workshops and program she has worked so hard to start. She is dedicated to making this program successful," answered Rachael. "Even the Warden and a few others could be in trouble. If someone is stealing drugs and selling them, they won't want to lose their income illegal or not."

"What are we supposed to do with this pill switching information? What can we do?" asked Lucinda.

"For now, probably nothing. We must take our cues from the Warden, Sharon and the police. We need to keep our eyes and ears open and our focus solely on the workshops. We have two serious problems going on. First is the murder and second is the drug mix-up. The police and Mrs. James have their hands full. We know that news travels fast among the inmates. Faulty or inaccurate speculation rather than truth is more likely taking place. It may very well happen that the inmates themselves solve both mysteries," remarked Brooksie.

"How about we change topics and get down to the personal stuff," suggested Lucinda. "Brooksie, the girls haven't heard about your date in Paradise."

Brooksie gave a short run down on the Paradise Ranch. She talked about the great food, the spectacular scenery, the hayride and all sorts of friendly animals to pet or just stare at. She didn't go into much detail about going to Luke's fine home, the wine, the dance, toe-tingling kiss and Luke's abrupt suggestion to take her home. "He did kiss me at my door and asked about another date for tomorrow night. Is he just fooling around with me? I don't know how to take him. What if he only wants a one-nighter? I really hate dating. It's more like a guessing game."

Her three friends roll their eyes and snicker ever so slightly. Anita advised her with a sweet smile, "I may be the youngest and the one with the least experience with men in this group, but I say just have fun and be yourself and see what unfolds."

"Great advice from our soon to be PhD companion," affirmed Rachael. "See you all next week and may we all stay safe with our Lancer's adventure."

"With a mischievous smile, Anita stepped in front of Rachael, blocking her way and said, "Aren't you going to tell the girls about your date with Roco Lagunta?"

"You little traitor. Anita. You would be a failure as a spy. You'd tell all without needing one second of persuasion. First, I need to give you a little, but lengthy background information. One of the inmates in our group, Susie Wu, was found guilty of premeditated murder of her violent husband. They'd been married for ten years. Susie had three miscarriages. The doctor said they were probably caused by the beatings from her husband. The last eight years of their marriage he beat her regularly and the injuries were more severe with each beating. Susie worked as a waitress, at the same place for the last five years. She was well liked by the other employees and the boss. Her husband was responsible for Susie loosing several jobs before this last one. She was the sole wage earner. Mr. Wu claimed some kind of disability. He simply stayed home and drank up her hard earned salary. She would often show up at work with visible bruises and twice with broken bones. She always said she was just too clumsy and always running into something. Her boss and the other waitresses many times told her about the women's shelter. They even invited her to move in with one of them. She never admitted she was being abused. It was like she was ashamed and terrified at the same time. Her husband would go to her workplace and make such a violent scene that her employer had no choice but to let her go for the safety of the customers and the other employees.

"Her husband's behavior was becoming more and more unpredictable and he began accusing her of having affairs with the cooks and the boss. During the last month, he was showing up at the restaurant, he would sit at the lunch counter for hours staring at the cooks, the boss and at Susie.

"Eventually, her boss sadly told her he would have to terminate her employment because of her husband's bizarre behavior. It was frightening everyone. After she returned home that night, she told her husband that he must stay away from her workplace or the boss was going to fire her.

"Apparently Mr. Wu said little that night, except to say he understood what was happening. She later told the police he was acting calm. He ate dinner in silence and went to bed at his usual time. Next morning she arrived at work at her usual shift time and was assigned to work the cash register. The boss was standing next to her when her husband walked in, parked himself directly in front of both of them, pulled out a gun and started yelling profanities. He was wild eyed, sweating and the gun in his hand was shaking. He kept swinging the gun around as people dove to the floor or headed for the door.

"The boss opened the drawer underneath the cash register. He looked directly into Susie's eyes then down to the open drawer. She followed his eyes down to the drawer and saw a gun. While her husband continued his threats to shoot everyone in sight and yelling, "You all must die" Susie gingerly picked up the gun and pulled the trigger two times. Mr. Wu immediately fell dead to the ground.

"The prosecutor claimed Susie knew all about the gun and planned to kill her husband. She had no money for a lawyer, no family, so one was assigned to her. Everyone she worked with were supportive and were witnesses for her. But unfortunately, no one had any extra finances to help her.

When Mr. Logunta heard about her case he asked if she would let him represent her and have her case reopened. He is working hard to get her a new trial and make it right.

"We have gone out for coffee several times, and once to dinner and a musical. He is a fine man and I enjoy what little time I have with him. Quit your snickering you three. Nothing serious just a date."

Brooksie broke the silence. "I, for one think a great deal of Mr. Lagunta. He has taken on two almost pro-bono cases for Houston and Wilamina in our group. He is fortunate Rachael, to know you. You are a treasure and a keeper. He deserves such a great woman."

"Stop it! You are going to make me blush. We have had only one real date so far. He hasn't asked me out for a second one, yet.. Brooksie, like you, I'm not crazy about the dating scene either. At least you know Luke's a great kisser."

Good-byes were said again and each one went their own way.

CHAPTER SIXTEEN

**"Good judgment comes from experience,
and a lot of that comes from bad judgment."**
Will Rogers (1879-1935)

Workshop #5

"Today we're going to begin our session with a word or two that have to do with any kind of addictions or other destructive behaviors," stated Lucinda. "Please call out your words and I'll write them on the board. Brooksie would you please start us off."

"Sure thing, Lucinda. Street drugs and lying."

"Sweets and other kinds of junk food and sleeping around," offered Corrina.

Houston yelled out, "Bad partners and picking the same old losers."

"Pain killers, cigarettes, blaming others and making excuses," offered Delores.

"I got some," sang out Wilamina. "Letting everyone put you down, hitting you or calling you names. That can be like an addiction. If you keep letting it happen over and over."

"Not taking medicine that helps you like my crazy ex-partner would always do. Laziness, anger, jealousy and cruelty are destructive. Cruelty is the worst one of all," shared Sammy. "I get all worked up every time I think about how she tortured my innocent dogs. Don't think I'll ever get over it."

Lucinda wrote a few of her own ideas upon the board: sex, sleeping too much, reacting without thinking about consequences, all work and no play, pity parties, denial, bad choices, giving up, procrastination, cowardly, anger and, resentment.

"We have lots of words on the board to think about. What have been your addictions? What behaviors have been the most destructive? What behaviors have brought you joy or good feelings about yourself. Which words have, brought you some success? Anyone like to start?" asked Lucinda.

"I can start," said Sammy. "My addictions are junk food, too much of it, lots of beer. Which, by the way, I miss. Maybe my dogs were an addiction, but a good one. I sure miss them. I think I became crazy as a youngster trying to make my folks love me. I would've been happy if they just liked me. After a while I did my best to make them miserable. I got poor grades in school, got in lots of fights, dressed like a slob. In my twenties I dressed like a guy, had a crew cut, even tied my boobs down with scarves. I know it drove them crazy and embarrassed the hell out of them. The only time I wasn't angry was when I was around my pets and my partner. But she went crazy and took it out on my pets. Those dogs were the only creatures who loved me." Sammy placed her arms in a self-hug position and stared into space.

Brooksie asked her, "Can you identify the behaviors you consider the most destructive?

"Making myself as ugly as possible to hurt my parents. I am gay, but not butch. I'm a woman and I'm okay with that. I'm simply attracted to other women. Never got hot looking at some guy. I'm me. I should have done the best I could just being me. Mr. Blackmore sees me as a good person, gay or straight, pretty or plain, just a person who loves animals. I'll probably always be sad my parents didn't want me around, but Dr. Blackmore wants me and I'll be the best damn assistant he's ever had. I'll make him proud."

"I think Mr. Blackmore is a wise man and sounds like he thinks the world of you. Your parents are the losers. Someday I'll have dogs and you can bet your life I'll bring them to your fine vet," remarked Houston.

Brookie added she agreed with Houston, as did several others in the group. "You will definitely be an asset to his practice. I've already spoken to my animal crazy aunt about Dr. Blackmore and his future assistant."

Sammy covered her face with her hands, but spread her fingers so she could peek. "You're embarrassing me. I'm not used to hearing anything good about myself. I like it."

"I've been addicted to every drug you can snort, swallow, inject or breathe in," boasted Corrina. "All have hurt my body and my mind. Having a baby was the best thing ever happened to me. I was so happy that day and then he died and my life ended. I've lost count with how many guys I've slept with and still no pregnant me. All that did was give me herpes, so I could hate myself even more. Since you've all pointed out I have a good memory, I'm going to start using it. I'm only thirty-eight. I have time to make changes. All my family and Jose's family turned against me and blamed me for my baby's death. I have felt like I'm worth nothing. At least when I was using I felt pretty good. Crazy as it sounds to me, I think some of the women in here have been nicer to me than anyone outside these walls."

Lucinda asked, "You've talked about signing up for classes offered in here. You still plan to do that?"

"Yes I've already spoken to the counselor and will start taking two classes soon. Something in the medical field. Maybe even in nursing. I could work in the hospital nursery and maybe God will be forced to forgive me for all my sins."

"I'm glad to hear you are opening up your options. Now you're taking steps to make your dream or goal of a better life for yourself come true. Congratulations, Corrina," confirmed Brooksie.

Jackie took a turn. "My parents treated me a lot like Sammy's folks treated her. I always felt like I didn't measure up to what they wanted, a girlie girl. I've spent years trying to make them pay for making me feel like something bad was wrong with me. I felt like I didn't belong in the family. I hoped for a long time I was adopted and one day my real parents would claim me. What a wasted dream that was.

"I've had my share of hangovers. Alcohol was my thing. I never got hooked on drugs. My nanny was my life saver. I could be honest with her and she was always accepting and encouraged me to find my niche in life. She tried many times to get me to go to AA meetings. I know she worried about my health, still does."

Lucinda inquired, "Have you attended any of the AA meetings offered here in prison?"

"No. I'm not drinking in here. Would if I could, just can't locate the Lancer's bar."

"You might find it helpful and even informative when you are released. Then you might decide to continue to attend an AA group on the outside." suggested Lucinda.

Jackie nodded, but remained silent.

"I think the same way like Corrina," said Berri. "The best time in my life was holding my sweet baby and watching him sleep. His murder took away all that was good from me. I can't shake the guilt about leaving Ali with Sam. I know you all say Sam did the killing, but I let Ali down.

"My addictions are too much food, and too much guilt, if that's possible."

"Berri, do you think you deserve to be happy and joyful?" asked Brooksie.

"No ma'am. The only time felt happy was being around Ali and at work. I got along good with the other employees and I liked pleasing and helping them old folks at the nursing home. They were always so grateful for whatever little thing I did for them. I'm missing some of them. Some didn't never have any visitors and that made me sad."

Sasha confronted the group, "You all think I'm a sex addict. Maybe I am, but I'm really addicted to living the good life and that takes money. Corrina you will always be an addict waiting for the next high. You only say what you want them goodie goodies to hear. At least I'm not a fucking hypocrite.

"What you think of me means nothing, because you are nothing." She flips the finger at Corrina.

Houston exclaimed, " Sasha you are one sorry bitch."

The discussions and comments continued up until 11:30 and reluctantly the group broke up.

CHAPTER SEVENTEEN

**"If you tell the truth, you
don't have to remember anything."**
Mark Twain, *Samuel Langhorne Clemens*
(1835-1910)

Ongoing investigation of Simone's murder.....

Detective Yamoto made arrangements with the Warden to meet again and with inmate Sharon Primm. It was decided to have the meeting in the Warden's office, because it was the most private place available. There was an apparent threat to Sharon that needed to be addressed. Brooksie informed Dr. James about Houston's warning concerning Sharon. Houston overheard inmates talking about Sharon and resenting her special position. She quoted, 'Just 'cause she got a doctor degree she thinks she's better than the rest of us. The time to bring her down to our level is coming.'

Detective Yomoto and his partner Detective Rowe were admitted to the Warden's office accompanied by the CO Ruby. She was the Warden's most trusted CO on the day shift. Sharon was brought to the office thirty minutes earlier by Ruby.

The Warden asked Sharon to repeat what Houston had overheard. Sharon complied and then handed the detectives three notes she received over the past few weeks.

"As you can see they are not dated and they are printed in a child-like manner. The first note read, 'nose out', the second one, 'you are not too smart for a doctor', and the last one, ' you can be the next Simone'. I'm not sure if this has anything to do with the pills that were analyzed. Simone had confided in Houston the pain meds the nurse, gave her did not relieve her pain. She didn't want to return to see Dr. Ronan because he made her uncomfortable and called him an octopus.

The Warden informed the detectives that just a day ago inmate Maxine Ritter, who sustained a suspicious looking bite mark, was given a so-called pain medication which apparently did not relieve any discomfort. I have the pills in my office, waiting to be sent off to the lab for analysis."

Detective Yomoto advised both ladies that the department has been made aware of the placeboes for quite a while. He also complimented Sharon on her observational skills and for reporting to the warden. "Would you be willing to continue your astute observations and report them, when possible, to Brooksie, Rachael or the Warden secretly?

"Absolutely. I'm concerned about the safety of the four social workers who are voluntarily running the workshops. They are making the pilot program possible and are receiving no financial compensation. Besides that, they are my best friends."

"I do appreciate your concerns, Sharon. We will keep an eagles watch over them. We do have safety valves in place for protection of those who might need it."

"You already know about the bite wound on Maxine's arm. Simone apparently bit her while they struggled." added Dr. James.

"That's correct Dr. James. As you know we have the report and have Maxine under surveillance." responded Detective Yamoto. "Now Sharon if you would please follow Detective Rowe to the next office, she has some questions for you."

After Sharon and the detective were gone, Detective Yamoto spoke about the undercover inmate. "I don't think it is going to take very long for our informant to come up with enough evidence against Miss Ritter, her accomplice and the other law breakers. Sorry about keeping her identity a secret, but we have good reasons for doing so. She is going to be able to pass coded notes to Sharon and to the social workers, Brooksie and Rachael.

"Also on your recommendation, the plant is aware of your trust of Dr. Gibran and her nurse, Mela Washington."

Detective Rowe and Sharon are summoned back to the front office. Sharon is also instructed about the informant whose identity needs to remain anonymous, and to tell no one that there is an undercover police person. In fact, no one is to know there is a undercover person anywhere in the prison. "I have a question," said Sharon. "How am I suppose to meet her?"

"You already have. When the time is right she will introduce herself to you. If someone hands you a note or if you find a note stuck inside your notebook and it reads, "Heads up", give it immediately to your warden or, to any of the four workshop ladies, Dr. Gibran or Mela Washington. This week we have added five new undercover CO's working for the police department. You can hand the note to them as well as the others. Do your best to act natural around them. Their names will be given to you later this week. You can give them the note as well. They will have on name tags just like all the other CO's.

I would suggest your informant stays away from Sasha," said Sharon, " It has been rumored she has somehow been in contact with Loreli Woods, or knows someone who is in contact with her. Loreli is supposedly locked up 23/24. She attempted to murder her husband while he was attending a divorce group at the Grief Clinic, where I used to work. My colleagues from the Grief Clinic are running the workshops here and refer Loreli as the Grief

Clinic's Black Widow. She is cunning, manipulative and will use anybody to get what she wants. The woman has zero conscience and at present is fighting extradition to England for the murder of her first husband. I'm sure your informant is smart, but Loreli is a talented and experienced psychopath."

"Thanks Dr. Primm," responded Detective Rowe. "We are aware of inmate Loreli Woods and she cannot cause us any problems, trust me. She is to be deported back to England in the near future to stand trial. Remember to trust only those we have told you to trust."

The Warden notified the front desk to send CO Ruby to her office to return Dr. Primm to her section.

All four shook hands and made plans to meet again in one week.

Morning in Dr. Ronan's office ....

The nurse was reading off the list of patients the doctor was to see this morning. "Loreil Woods is on the schedule again doctor. What are her recurring problems?"

"She has terrible headaches of unknown origin. I can't seem to figure out the best treatment or drugs that would possibly help her for any length of time. My listening to her concerns does give her a little temporary relief. After all she is in solitary most of the time and that would make anybody needy for human contact."

"I know how seductive some are," the nurse answered under her breath and out of ear shot of her boss.

Loreli and Delores were sitting next to each other. An inattentive guard was standing next to Loreli. The two inmates were whispering back and forth.

Loreli whispered, "I know I've told you this before, but I'm going to say it again. Watch your back with Sharon Primm and the social workers. Especially with Brooksie. They set me up over a year ago and now you see where I am. If they don't like you they'll screw you over. We'd all better off if Sharon was out of the picture and would take the four spying facilitators with her. You're a smart girl. Put the word out on Sharon and then on her cohorts. Those workshops are stirring up a lot of shit around here. Sharon kisses the Warden's ass and they are getting to be buddies, if you know what I mean. Don't say I didn't warn you sister."

Before Delores could verbally respond, the nurse called her to the doctor's office. She only remained in his office for a few minutes and as she was leaving the infirmary she walked by Loreli and winked at her. Delores was holding or palming a small vial.

Janet, in a surly voice said, "You're up Loreli and please remember there are many others waiting to see the doctor."

Loreli gave the nurse a hands up signal with one hand the middle finger salute with the other.

CHAPTER EIGHTEEN

**"Down in their hearts, wise men know this truth:
the only way to help yourself is to help others."**
Elbert Hubbard, in *The Philistine*

Workshop #6

"Good morning," said Brooksie. "Today's workshop topic is support options when in and out of prison. Honest support comes from those who have no agenda, other than wanting you to find your place in the world. Choose people who only want what is best for you, what will keep you healthy, safe, working towards your potential in a constructive way. The goal is to develop a sense of pride in yourself, this is not the same as being prideful. Never forget you are not superior or inferior, you are simply a human with strengths and weaknesses. You earn self-respect by struggling with your flaws and increasing your strengths. This is how you build character. Choose carefully the people you listen to. Look at their character. Are they dependable? Do their actions speak louder than their words? Watch what they do and then decide if their advice makes sense. Does it sound true?"

Lucinda took over, " I'm going to call your name and ask you to give the first name or names of people you believe offer this kind of support.

"Houston."

"My lawyer, my brothers, Sharon and Willy. Guess I'd add you two facilitators."

"Jackie."

"Mrs. Slauson on the outside. Sharon and Mela Washington in here."

"Char."

"My brother."

"Wilamina."

"Houston's lawyer, Sharon, Houston and Dr. Gibran and Mela. I would want you and Brooksie.."

"Corrina."

"No one. Maybe Sharon and Houston."

"Berri."

"Houston and Willy. Oh hell everyone in this group is okay by me. I'd ask Houston and Willy first and then the rest of you."

"Delores."

"My parents and minister."

"Sammy."

"Dr. Blackmore, Houston, Willy and Mary, my outside friend, and probably you and Brooksie."

"Sasha."

"My uncle and my pimp, John."

"Luella."

"My dad and all of you guys."

After each inmate identified the person or persons they thought would be part of their support, a general discussion took up the next two hours. The group as a whole tried to dissuade Sasha from considering her pimp as someone who wanted the best for her.

Sasha laughed heartily and said, "You're all just wishing you had my outside contacts. John is my ace in the hole. He treats me right and together we make a great team."

"Delores, would it be possible for you to consider a third person. One who you know is not judgmental of you, maybe someone who has more of a neutral nature?" asked Brooksie.

Delores hesitated momentarily then looked at Sharon through piercing eyes, "I pick Sharon. I believe I could tell her my most inner thoughts, no matter how depraved or disgusting and she wouldn't pass judgment." Sharon made brief eye contact with Dee and nodded ever so slightly.

The group continued to share their ideas and opinions who would be the best person or persons to give fair and wise suggestions and support. Brooksie reminded them about the counselors available in the prison and when they are released, counselors are often found at colleges and universities that could be affordable. Check out different churches. They may offer counseling as well. Doctor's offices may also be a source of information. They may have a list of therapists they would refer you to.

....

The Warden was waiting outside the mess hall after the workshop ended. She spoke with Lucinda and Brooksie and asked them if they could return to the prison on Saturday to meet with her. She asked if they would get in touch with the other two facilitators and arrange for them to also come to the meeting. "We will meet in the library at 10 a.m."

Saturday ....
The four showed up a little before 10 o'clock Saturday morning and headed for the prison library where the Warden was waiting.

"Thank you for coming. I know this must be inconvenient for you all especially since you're not on anyone's payroll. I want to go over the instructions you received last week and to see if you have any questions or concerns." She went over the passing of a note that says "Heads up" and the safe group of people they would need to pass it on too immediately.

Anita started to write down the names, but was quickly told that was not needed. The Warden explained the absolute necessity for secret keeping because of the danger to all the undercover workers if their identity became public knowledge. "Are any of you concerned you won't be able to act in a normal way around the undercover CO's?" Sharon is also privy to the same information you all have and will also have to act her usual self."

No one spoke for a while, not even sounds of breathing could be heard. Anita began to sniffle and whispered, "I'm so afraid for Sharon."

"I understand your concerns and fears for your dear friend, but we need to hide our emotions and work hard doing the workshops. I do believe Detective Yomoto when he told me the department is very close to solving the murder and ending the illegal drug activities. Can you all pull this necessary deception off? I know this isn't what you signed up for but you will be helping to improve prison life for the inmates. I apologize for these unfortunate turn of events especially for my apparent ignorance to what's been going on."

Animated discussion followed for the next hour. There was a general agreement by everyone that they would do what was asked. "How will we know who those five CO's are besides just their name tags? Some of the CO's don't wear tags." asked Brooksie.

"Good question. They are all new guards, new employees to the prison. I've brought pictures with me. They will always wear their name tags. Take your time looking at these pictures. Once you've memorized their faces, I will destroy them in my office. Their names are Sheri, Rosita, Jesse, Aula and Bart.

The group studied the faces on the pictures and repeated the names. They agreed it would be best if they didn't talk about the undercover activity any time or any place or with anyone including family.

Some brief, but serious hugging took place outside the library and then the four started for home.

Wilamina and Houston..............

Wilamina asked Houston, "Did you really mean what you said this morning about me being part of your support thing?"

"Hell yes. You've got a big mouth, but a big heart too. I'm thinking about when I get out of here. I don't want the old life. I want to have a chance at a real life. I want my own place, make money on my terms, depend only on myself. I've been reading about private investigators. I think I'd be good at investigating and catching dirt bags and knowing they're off the streets. How about you? You really consider me as a good support?" inquired Houston.

"Yeah, I do. You're the first white face I trust. You're not a homo are you?"

"Damn you Willy, you really got to ask me that? I like big guys, if you know what I mean. Don't tell me you're into the females."

"No way. Sorry I asked. Meant no harm or disrespect. Thanks again for helping me get a lawyer. Last week, he told me he believes he can help me get another trial or maybe a judge will sign some kind of paper and I will get out of this hole. Mr. Lagunta said I was not guilty of manslaughter. I defended by brother and that's all I was doing. He also told me he thought I was very brave."

Houston added, "Looks like we both have a chance to get a new trial, or whatever it takes to get our sentences reversed. I'm working hard with my business class. I want to be ready when they open those gates to start running my own life."

Wilamina asked in a questioning sort of way with her eyes looking at her feet, "Maybe we could work together, you'd be boss of course and we could call our business Salt and Pepper."

Houston roared and grabbed Wilamina and held her in a bear hug, "Salt and Pepper, I love it. Guess we're already partners, Pepper."

CHAPTER NINETEEN

**"Courage is doing what you're afraid to do.
There can be no courage unless you're scared."**
Eddie Rickenbacker

The dinner hour had just begun for the women locked up in Lancer's prison. Sharon excused herself from the group she usually hung out with. "I've got to make a potty stop before I indulge in tonight's gourmet meal."

Sharon left the cafeteria area and headed for the restroom followed by two other inmates and a CO. As soon as the three entered into the bathroom, yelling and fight-like sounds were coming from the cafeteria. The CO left her position at the restroom and ran back to the cafeteria area to assist other guards.

The minute the CO took off running, the inmates who had accompanied Sharon began to attack her. They moved in tandem. The two, well-trained in the martial arts, and systematically beat Sharon. They started hitting her head then moved down her body. Sharon did her best to defend herself, but she was no match for the likes of them. She barely felt the slip of the cold steel in her back before she fell to the floor unconscious.

The fight broke out, in the cafeteria, about the same time Sharon headed for the restroom. Houston watched Sharon head for the door then saw the two trouble-making inmates follow her in. Houston whispered to Wilamina, "Time to go to the ladies room, Willy. I smell a rat. Something is up and it's not good for Sharon."

Wilamina immediately joined her new friend, but they were both stopped by the CO. "Ladies you will have to wait your turn."

"I can't wait ma'am. I have peeing problem and the doc can't seem to figure out. Please let me go, " begged Houston with clenched fists.

At that moment, a deafening commotion started at one of the long tables. Plastic plates, cups and even benches were flying through the air. A number of inmates were going at each other, pulling out snatches of hair that had been colored one too many times. Profanities, usually attributed to sailors, flooded the huge room. Whistles were blown and the alarm system was activated. Soon there were a dozen or more CO's working hard to get the free-for-all under control.

Houston and Willy took advantage of the chaos and made a beeline for the door racing to the rest room. Willy flung the door open and leaped on the closest inmate and began to beat her around the head. Sharon's limp and bloody body was under the other two inmates. They were taking turns hitting her about the head and chest. Houston grabbed a saliva-spitting inmates, and banged her head on the floor. Houston growled like a wild animal, knocked one of the inmates unconscious with one blow of her fist and quickly started on the other one that Wilamina had been pummeling.

Back in the cafeteria, Sasha had also watched Sharon leaving the cafeteria for the restroom with two tough inmates. She thought to herself how odd the CO didn't stay with them. Then chaos in the cafeteria began in earnest, and all hell broke loose. She tried to race toward the restroom to see if there was a problem brewing. But she was roughly turned back by CO Rank Johnson.

Rank became quickly distracted by the fights going on and Sasha was able to run to the restroom. Soon as she opened the door she witnessed Houston and Wilamina pounding away on the two other inmates. Sharon was lying in a pool of blood and not moving.

Sasha screamed for the guards and a doctor. An alarm had already by screeching because of the cafeteria free-for-all. Sasha grabbed one of the guards as she was running toward the mess hall and soon more help arrived.

The two who had been savagely beating on Sharon were saved from further damage by four guards. The attackers of Sharon were dragged away and placed in isolation to await medical treatment.

Houston, wild-eyed and bloody screamed, "Get the damn doctor here now. Those animals were trying to kill Sharon. Call the Warden and the police. Help her, do you hear me, they were bent on killing her."

Wilamina had freed herself from one of the CO's and was cradling Sharon in her strong arms. "You going to be okay, you hear me. You hang on." Sharon weakly squeezed Willy's hand.

The riot was quickly contained. Sharon had been taken to the infirmary awaiting an ambulance. Dr. Gibran rendered emergency treatment, stopped most of the facial bleeding and discovered a back wound. She said out loud to no one in particular that Sharon's vitals were better than she had expected. Sharon faded in and out of consciousness.

An hour or so later, the Warden met up with Sharon's emergency doctor in the hospital. She quickly notified Detective Yomoto, Brooksie and Rachael of the attack.

Soon after..............
As soon as Detective Yomoto and his partner got the word about the fight and the attack on Sharon, they hot-footed

themselves to the hospital with their siren turned on. They quickly met up with the Warden and the emergency room doctor.

Dr. Swann informed the anxious group, "Sharon sustained a broken nose, a concussion, fractured left arm and two cracked ribs. There is a stab wound in her back which amazingly missed any vital organs or vessels. The bleeding from the wound is minimal. She took a pretty good pounding, but it seems her friends got to her in time and put an end to the beating. The two perpetrators are being treated for non life-threatening injuries, and several broken bones. One may have some internal damage. We will need to keep them under observation for a day or two. I understand, Warden, they will be kept in isolation and under guard as long as they are here?"

"That is true. As soon as possible, I would like them returned to prison. When you feel it would be medically safe to return them, please have someone let me know. I'm anxious to question them and get them back under lock and key. They made a brutal attempt on Sharon's life. There will be charges against them. Isn't that correct Detective Yomoto?"

"You are correct Warden. Dr., would it be possible for us to question them today?"

"Unfortunately, no. They are heavily sedated. One has a broken wrist and nose. The other one sustained a broken nose, a dislocated shoulder and a broken jaw with possible internal damage. They will both need surgical intervention. Tomorrow morning would be a better time to speak with them."

"How about Houston and Wilamina, the two who saved Sharon from being murdered?" asked the detective.

The doctor responded, "The two ladies that intervened for Sharon sustained very little damage, only a few bruises. I wouldn't mind having the two of them watching my back if I ever felt myself threatened or jumped on."

"They both think highly of Dr. Primm. She has been trying to improve the lives of inmates, even though she too is an inmate." added the Warden.

Dr. Swann left the room and the three talked over a few details concerning the attack. "Who else is in danger now? asked the exhausted looking Warden. The dark circles under her eyes were growing darker and getting deeper with each passing day.

Before they could answer, Malina the assistant to the warden came rushing in, nearly out of breath, she said, "I'm not at all surprised at this development, Jealousy has raised its head. I told you that some of the inmates felt Sharon was receiving special attention."

"You may be correct about the jealously aspect, but I'm beginning to believe there may be a more sinister motive involved." contended the Warden.

"What are you suggesting Florence, Dr. James,?" confronted Malina. "What do you plan to do with Houston and Wilamina? It is my understanding they both had to be subdued by several guards."

"Not sure at this very moment, but I will see to it they are recognized as heroes and receive some type of award or reward."

Malina responded in a challenging tone, "How can you be sure they didn't have a part in getting the riot started? Perhaps they were part of the plan for distracting the COs. You do remember how devious the prison population can be, don't you?"

"Malina we'll talk later. Right now you are needed back at the prison. You do remember you are my assistant?"

The assistant, obviously upset, begrudgingly leaves the hospital corridor.

After Malina was out of hearing range, Detective Rowe asked the Warden, "How well do you know your assistant?"

"A thorough background check was done and she appeared fine. We have different goals for the incarcerated and her opinion of the women is quite jaded. She is bright and a hard worker, but we do butt heads on occasion."

"To answer your question about safety of others I will say we are concerned about you, the facilitators, possibly Dr. Gibran and her nurse, Mela. Sharon was a surprise. It's beginning to look like there is more than a drug problem going on here. Is there a possibility the Sharon's program is possibly in jeopardy?"

"If the facilitators are endanger of becoming targets of violence, then the workshops will have to be shut down. Sharon, Brooksie and Rachael were responsible for sending the suspicious drugs to a lab. I didn't know your department was already looking into the questionable drugs and Dr. Ronan and his nurse."

"We are close to making arrests. Our months of surveillance are beginning to pay off. Sorry, I'm not at liberty to share any further details at this time. I want to remind you about changing everyday patterns including driving to and from work and to remind the others how important changing patterns are. Keep an eye out for each other and report anything that seems unusual and out of character. The note that may be passed with the code word may be the key to solving many questions and lead us to all of the perpetrators."

CHAPTER TWENTY

**"I give you bitter pills in sugar coating. The pills
are harmless: the poison is in the sugar."**
Stanislaw Lee

The next day following the riot and the attack on Sharon, Malina requested a meeting with Dr. Ronan. They agreed to meet in one of the unoccupied visitor's rooms. They seated themselves in a corner and the doctor whispered, "When can we meet at our place. I can't stand looking at you and not being able to enfold you with my arms and legs?"

She whispered back, "Are you crazy! Eyes and ears of the police are everywhere now, because you got so fucking greedy and horny."

"Greedy you say, you always push me to bring in more. You know I'm wildly in love with you. I'll do anything to please you. Have you started the divorce proceedings like you promised?"

"Mitchell, you are a fool. I took the first step and now Sharon will be making the hospital her home for some time. The pressure needs to stay on those four goody goodies and Sharon's program needs to end. Are you keeping your roving eye closely on your smitten nurse? You need to keep the money coming in. Janet is key to keeping the drugs moving. As long as she thinks she has a chance with you, she'll keep on turning a blind eye.

"For now, I don't think we should tempt fate and see each other away from Lancers. We don't need to flirt with suspicion. My stupid husband is an important part of our plan. He is going to help us soon, unbeknownst to him. I'm going to have him throw a scare into the facilitators. We've got to watch our backs. I'm reminding you again, don't trust Gibran or her nurse. They've been asking too many questions lately and have been talking to the warden. Keep your nose clean and especially keep your hands of any of the young inmates."

"What the hell are you talking about? Who've you been listening to?"

"Don't fart around with me, Mitchell. I hear all the rumors and I know about your lack of control and sleazy reputation. Don't bother to deny it, just stop it."

"You have no room to talk Missy, you've been known to switch sides whenever convenient."

"I do what I have to do to reach my goal. You on the other hand follow wherever your other head leads."

"I'm led right to you, but you cut me off too many times."

"You still sleep in the same bed with your pitiful, gullible wife? Use her for a change or not. But whatever you do just keep it in your pants when not at home."

CHAPTER TWENTY-ONE

**"I've learned......That sometimes all a person needs
is a hand to hold and a heart to understand."**
Andy Rooney

Brooksie picked up Anita and they drove to the hospital to visit Sharon. The Warden had informed Brooksie of the attack and she passed on the terrible news to the others. She knew how close Anita and Sharon were so decided to tell her about Sharon's close call face to face. She located Anita at the university and together they made the trip to the hospital.

Anita tearfully talked of her admiration and love or her mentor and mother figure, Sharon. Brooksie listened quietly, thinking over her own fears for her friend, Sharon and the others. *How many of us could be in danger? Is there a connection between shutting down Sharon's program and the illegal sale of drugs? There must be more than one rotten apple scheming and willing to do the dirty work. Dr. Ronan and probably his nurse are the two most likely suspects in the drug trade. Who wants the workshops to fail? Doesn't seem possible the Warden could be trying to sabotage the program.* "We need to keep our heads clear. We need to remain vigilant and report anything suspicious to the Warden or the detectives," said Brooksie out loud for her benefit as well as for Anita's.

"I'll keep it together when we see Sharon," responded Anita. "I know she would want us to be strong and if possible keep the program intact."

They pulled into the hospital parking lot and walked into the emergency room. The detectives and Dr. Gibran greeted them. "We were just talking with Dr. Swann, Sharon's doctor. He is going to set her broken arm and take care of her nose this afternoon. She will be under observation for another forty-eight hours for any other problems that may arise from the head injuries or the stabbing. She sustained a concussion, so far it only seems minor. She has been talking with the nurses about the workshops and wants them to continue, but has great concern for the welfare of the four facilitators."

Anita asked to see her. They followed the doctor to her room. Two policemen were posted outside her room. The minute Anita caught sight of her friend, she yelled out, "How could anyone do this to you?"

"Calm yourself dear, I know how terrible I look, but I'm sure all will heal up completely and quickly. My arm may take a little time. Thank God it's my left arm."

Walking to the other side of the bed Brooksie placed her hand gently on Sharon's shoulder. "We are going to keep our schedule for the workshops. We believe it is important for the sake of the inmates."

"I'm afraid for all of you. I don't think this is only about the workshops. There's got to be more at stake than the program. The illegal drug trade must also have something to do with this."

"I agree, the four of us will be meeting with the Warden and the detectives tomorrow. It is my understanding the police also have some plans they want to share with us. They've already put safety measures in place for you and for us. Sharon, do you know the two women who attacked you?"

"I've seen them around, like in the mess hall, but I've never spoken with them. Maybe Houston or Willy know more?" I suppose you know those two saved my life."

"Yes and I'll never be able to thank them enough. They are both heroes," affirmed Anita.

"Rest now and try not to worry. Focus on healing. For your safety, the visitor list is short. Most of the inmates in your workshops send their best wishes and prayers. By the way, your rescuers did quite a number on the attackers. In fact, they are in much worse shape than you. I'm thankful Houston and Willy are on our side. Much to everyone's surprise Sasha, also tried to help you. She was stopped by a CO. Who would think little Miss Ho would be one of your defenders. Bye for now."

CHAPTER TWENTY-TWO

**"When you get to the end of your rope,
tie a knot and hand on."**
Anonymous

Workshop #7

The four facilitators rode together to the prison. This was Brooksie's and Lucinda's scheduled day. They decided since a meeting had been scheduled for the four of them with the Warden and the detectives for 1:00 p.m., it would be easier and safer to travel together.

The miles raced by as the women shared concerns, suspicions and ideas for the long drive. "Is it a coincidence or fate that the workshop topics for today are road blocks, making changes and self-change?" quizzed Lucinda. "I wonder how much our group will know about Sharon."

"They probably know far more than we do. The communication in prison is unbelievably immediate and from what I've heard it's fairly accurate. Whatever the reason, I'm glad we can give them a real life example of roadblocks and changes!" expressed Brooksie.

The team entered the cafeteria and were met by the Warden and her assistant, Malina Smithers. The Warden addressed the group, "We have been giving your group an update on Sharon. I heard that two of you visited Sharon last night and have seen first-hand how quickly Sharon is recovering. We are not sure just exactly when she will be returning."

"That's correct," responded Brooksie. Sharon looks mighty beat up, but her spirits are great. She's in some pain, which is under control with meds. She assured us that she will be back in the saddle again soon."

The Warden continued, "The two attackers will be returned when the doctors give the okay. That's going to be awhile. They both sustained some serious injuries. They will, of course, remain in isolation both there and when they are returned to us here. The two are facing serious assault charges and will eventually go to trial. Any questions?"

Delores asked, "Have they talked about their motives for the attack? And are others involved? I've heard jealousy could be a motive."

"Obviously jealousy was one of the motives. Sharon's workshops have stirred up emotions. I can't say I'm really surprised by the events." responded Malina.

"I don't believe that for one second, " countered Houston. "It's More likely that greed has more to do with it than jealousy!"

"We'll leave you now to carry on with your workshop." said the Warden addressing the group. See you ladies at 1 p.m.

Rachael and Anita sat themselves at a bench away from the group. Anita informed the inmates that they were taking the role of observers today and will facilitate their workshop next Wednesday as usual.

Brooksie began, "We are all upset about Sharon. But we are eternally grateful to Houston and Wilamina for their heroic intervention. I also want to thank Sasha who also made an attempt to save Sharon from further harm."

Sasha remained quiet and stone faced. "Yeah, you can throw a mean punch. Guess if you want to stay alive as a ho you better know how to protect yourself. Right Sasha?" added Wilamina.

"You got that right, Blackie," answered Sasha with a barely noticeable grin.

Lucinda asked the women if anyone wanted to withdraw from the program. "We can see there are some safety issues. We will understand and if later you would like to join the program you'll be most welcomed."

No one stirred. Sammy spoke up, "I'm more determined than ever to learn how to improve myself. The attack on Sharon just pisses me off. Wish I could've left my mark on those bitches along with Tex and Willy."

"Okay let's get started." confirmed Brooksie. "Today we had planned to cover roadblocks and making changes. The attack on Sharon could present us with a huge roadblock. if we let it. It is possible that someone wanted to sabotage the program or is it about the program at all?

Sasha spoke up, "Maybe the murder of Simone and the attempt on Sharon's life are connected?"

"I'm thinking along the same lines," responded Lucinda. "The police department is working hard on different theories and are taking this attack very seriously."

"We are going to give you a few minutes to think about two questions: 1. What road blocks you have run into here in prison as well as outside of prison. 2. What future challenges do you think you might face?"

Brooksie and Lucinda took turns summarizing the obstacles members identified. Some brought up relapsing from alcohol and/or drugs, the same kind of destructive partners, crime ridden neighborhoods, old eating habits and not standing up to do what they knew to be right. They shared the difficulties in keeping up their appearances and health. Several talked about making impossible goals for themselves, followed by failure after failure, and spiraling down into old destructive patterns. Most inmates agreed they never felt they had any talent, or had any chance to make a better life for themselves. They continued to feel valueless, worthless and doomed to repeat the same mistakes over and over. Lack of power and sense of hopelessness were brought up.

Lucinda reminded the women if someone wanted them to do something illegal, harmful, dangerous, or cruel in any way they were their own first and best line of defense. "Don't bother to walk away. Run like hell in the other direction or stand and fight, your choice. Remember all fights don't have to be physical. Refusing to be sucked into doing something you don't want to do is fighting for yourself. You deserve to have someone in your corner because you are worth it."

As the workshop came to an end, Houston reminded the facilitators to "watch their backs."

The Warden appeared at the doorway and herded Brooksie and the other three into her office. The two detectives were already seated and Dr. Gibran was the last to enter.

Detective Yomoto looked at the upturned faces of the all-woman gathering and stated, "I'm truly a lucky man to have this many beautiful women, quietly waiting to hear me speak. My wife is not the listening type. Back to business, we've had a break. Shilo and Martha are talking. They claim they were approached by the CO Rank Johnson and offered cash and drugs to 'finish off' Sharon. They were to receive $250.00 each, $50.00 a month would be placed anonymously into their accounts. They would also receive drugs of their choice once every month.

"A warrant was issued to investigate Rank Johnson's home. The inspection revealed a large cache of illegal drugs, hidden in his basement. He has been arrested and is impatiently sitting in jail awaiting a court date. With the Warden's help, we have kept his arrest secret. We put out a rumor that states he is on sick leave and it is not known when he will return. No one, but the Warden and the five of you are privy to this information. I should add there are several in our department who are also privy.

"Now for our plan. We are working on Mr. Johnson to give us more information. He seems to be the type who likes to negotiate. We have Dr. Ronan and his nurse under observation.

"Each of you must take precautions. Report anything out of the ordinary. As I have instructed you before, but bears repeating, take different routes to come to the prison or going home and to your office, Change your routine, always travel in pairs, your keep cell phone charged and with you, Keep your gas tanks full and never hesitate to call us, anytime! Any questions?"

""Are you suggesting we may be in harms way, even when we are away from Lancers? Could our families be in any danger? asked the Warden.

Detective Rowe answered, "We are being overly cautious. Please keep your guard up at home, at work or wherever you happen to be. We are close to tying up this investigation, fingering and arresting the culprits. But, until then, please play it safe!"

The Warden looked around the room and addressed the facilitators, "If you all want to stop the workshops, I will understand, maybe it would be best."

Brooksie didn't hesitate for a moment, "Speaking for myself, I say no way should we stop the workshops. This pilot program is important for all prisoners throughout the U.S."

"It would break Sharon's heart if the program ceased. I have no intention of quitting," added Anita.

Rachael and Lucinda nodded enthusiastically in agreement.

"So, it's settled. The weekly workshops will continue. Remember you can change your minds at any time. Thank you all for what you are doing in these trying circumstances."

Detective Rowe mentioned the four new CO's, and possibly a fifth, that have been loaned out to the prison population. They are actually undercover cops. One of them-possibly two- will always be on duty. if it deems to be necessary." She reminded them of the names of the undercover CO's.

"I'm grateful for the added protection. It will be easy enough to explain their presence as hired staff for safety issues. No one will know they are actually police." advised the Warden.

Brooksie asked why Mrs. Smithers, the assistant, was not included in the meeting.

"Good question," responded Detective Yamoto. "We are in the process of digging further into her background as well as that of a few other employees. This information is not to be passed on. For the record, I'm not saying Ms. Smithers is a suspect. Please be cautious with what you say to anyone. There will be a few questions about this meeting and why certain people were not invited. Your answers should be brief. All you know is that you were invited to talk about Sharon's program and answer questions about continuing the program."

The Warden shook her head with a far-away look in her eyes. New wrinkles seemed to have appeared on her forehead overnight. Her eyes also seemed to have appeared even more sunken than before. The meeting ended with all participants shaking hands. The office quickly emptied.

Malina Smithers was standing in the hall when the detectives and the others left the Warden's office.

The Warden, wide-eyed, rushed over to her and tried to keep herself from stammering she said, "I thought you were taking a vacation day today?"

"I changed my mind this morning because my plans fell through. I thought there was no sense using up a day off for no good reason. What's going here with the police and the facilitators?"

The Warden could barely find enough saliva to wet her mouth so she faked a coughing fit, bought herself a little time while she thought up her answer.

"It was called by Detective Yomoto to stress the importance of reporting anything out of the ordinary and to always remain with a partner. I also talked about the program and let the ladies know that they could cancel anytime they felt it necessary for safety reasons. Dr. Gibran came early to attend the meeting and will pass on the safety tips to Dr. Ronan and others."

"I'm surprised you didn't inform me, Florence. We both need to be on the same page. I have the feeling I'm not as informed as I have a right to be. What's going on?"

"Malina you can talk directly with the detectives any time, by just picking up the phone. You have the same phone number that I have so please feel free to direct any and all of your questions to them.

"We have a serious problem on our hands. One murdered inmate and an attempted murder of another. The police are in charge and they are running the investigation their way. They tell us what they think we need to know. Now you must excuse me. I have much to do and the day will soon be over."

The assistant glared at the Warden's backside, started to say something, but changed her mind and abruptly walked away.

The Warden thought to herself, *That woman makes me nervous. I bet she rules her husband with an iron hand. He looked like a body builder, all muscled up, but with the resistance of a newborn, all show and no go, when it comes to standing up for himself.*

CHAPTER TWENTY-THREE

"Keep violence in the mind
Where is belongs."
Brian Aldiss, *"Charteris"*

The rain was coming down in sheets making visibility poor and the road slick. The four friends were driving back to their office after finishing up the 7th workshop and the meeting with the Warden and the detectives.

Earlier, they had agreed to go home their usual way because of the bad weather and Brooksie would be driving on a more familiar road.

"Next time we can take a different way home like the detectives recommended. I plan to follow their warnings to be more cautious and observant, but I can't imagine anyone attempting to hurt us," shared Lucinda.

Rachael chimed in, "I've been thinking a lot about who would most benefit from if our workshops coming to a halt?

"The Warden's assistant doesn't seemed thrilled with the workshops, however the Warden is very excited about the prospect of improving the lives of the inmates while they are in prison and when they get out," remarked Brooskie" Dr. Gibran also encourages personal responsibility and the importance of making constructive changes. From the rumors

I've heard, Dr. Ronan may be abusing the younger patients and possibly selling drugs. He would definitely be better off with us out of his hair. Whatever disgusting behaviors and illegal business he may be involved in, is being threatened by giving the inmates a voice. Sharon, the Warden, Dr. Gibran and her nurse, plus the four of us seem to be stirring up the pot. Even Janet, Dr. Ronan's nurse could be involved. She has been with the doctor for a while. Also, there might be a few inmates who might feel a lot better if we weren't around."

"I'm on the same page," said Lucinda in a serious tone. Simone was apparently killed because she knew something was terribly wrong. Houston told Sharon she believed that Simone's death was connected to Dr. Ronan."

It had been raining lightly when the group took off from the prison, but now it was raining seriously. Enough so that Brooksie turned on her windshield wipers.

The driver and her passengers had been so occupied with the serious conversations that they failed to notice a truck racing up behind them and quick as a wink began ramming them with force from behind. A scream flew out of Lucinda' mouth as their car was hit, from behind, several times. The force of the impact was enough to send them sliding off the wet road and into a clump of trees. Brooksie was able to maintain control of the steering wheel. She avoided hitting the thick trunk of an evergreen, luckily, the high brush brought the car to a halt. Both airbags deployed and the seat belts held all four passengers tight. No one spoke for a moment until Lucinda began to whimper. "My glasses broke and my nose hurts. What the hell happened? A drunken driver?"

Brooksie caught her breath, opened her door and looked up at the road. She looked for the truck, but saw no other cars on the road. She leaned back in the car and checked the condition of the others. Lucinda was bleeding quite a bit from the gash over her nose. She complained of feeling like she was going to throw up and clumsily got out of her side of the car and lowered herself to her knees and vomited. By now the other two passengers had freed themselves from their seat belts and moved stiffly to get out of the car.

"What the hell just happened? Did anyone see the driver or anything else?" cried out Rachael.

"It was a yellow truck, looked almost new. It looked like a man driving. Anita, you okay? You look pretty pale?" asked Brooksie.

"Yes. I'm still shaking. I've never been in a car accident before."

Brooksie pronounced, "That was no accident. The son-of-a rat hit us twice on purpose. I'm dialing 911. Lucinda you look like the only one who is hurt. How do you feel now?

"Hello, my name is Brooksie Everett and I'm reporting an accident, possibly an attempted murder. Our car was rammed twice, from behind by a big yellow truck. The driver did not stop. We need assistance. Please notify Detectives Yomoto and Rowe of the Homicide Department. No, I don't believe we need an ambulance, but my car is badly damaged. Also, if possible, please notify Warden James of Lancer's Prison about the attempt. There are four of us needing transportation and one may need to make a trip to the emergency room. Yes, we are on Sweeney Road about twenty-five miles south of the prison. Please hurry! We may still be in danger."

Lucinda was shivering when she stood up after heaving. Anita, using water from a bottle and her scarf, gingerly cleaned the blood off of her friend's face.

Brooksie was starting to stiffen up from the impact. She leaned back into the car and with much effort opened the consul and extracted a knife.

"What the f--- are you doing with that?" asked Rachael.

"'I don't know if the truck stopped or where the driver is, but I know that was an intentional hit. I think we all need to hide ourselves in the trees over there and wait for the police. That guy could come back and not for our autographs." They huddled together and slowly moved in tandem into a fairly dense spot of young trees. Seemed like hours before they heard a siren. Brooksie and Rachael cautiously ran up to the road to wave down the rescuers. It was Detective Yomoto and two other policemen who arrived first, followed by an ambulance.

Detective Yomoto raced out of his car and down the embankment. "I'm so glad to see all four of you standing. I've got to admit, my heart missed several beats when I got the call. Can you answer a few questions after the paramedics have done their magic?"

"You bet detective." replied Brooksie.

One of the policemen said to Brooksie, "You might want to let me hold your knife for you while you talk with the detective." He held out his hand and she skakily placed it handle first in his waiting gloved hand.

"I don't want you to think I'm a knife traveling serial killer. I keep it for emergencies like cutting the seat belt off just in case it gets stuck. I've heard of that happening. So I keep a knife nearby."

"May I ask what you had planned for your knife this time?" asked the Detective, making a poor attempt at hiding a grin.

"Go ahead and laugh, but I wasn't sure if that damn killer was going to come back. I don't guess you have ever encountered four frightened, angry women and one good sized knife. We are a team and we had a plan."

"Would you tell us about your plan?" asked the Detective snickering.

"Someday Detective Yomoto. Maybe someday." she answered straight-faced.

The ambulance crew finished cleaning up Lucinda's face with instructions for her to see her doctor as soon as possible. The rest were all given the ok sign. Then Brooksie gave her report to the awaiting detective. "It was a deliberate attempt by the driver to hurt us. I didn't spot his truck in my rear view mirror till the last few seconds before the impact. He was coming fast and straight for us. I couldn't see his face, but I could see that he had short hair under a cap. I tried to control my car with little success. At least we didn't hit the big tree trunk we were aimed at. It was a big yellow, new-like truck. We were flying off the road into the trees. Seemed like slow motion. Next came the air bags which hurt like hell, by the way."

The other three also told what little information they had. They recalled a, yellow, fairly new truck and a white man driving. It was agreed, that there would probably be some dents in his front bumper and maybe some silver paint from Brooksie's car. Due to the damage to the front and her bent wheels, her car was going to be towed back to Whitefall.

The facilitators were driven to the Grief Clinic. The police waited while Lucinda's husband arrived to take her to the emergency room. When Tony came racing through the clinic's door, his face was pale and his eyes were red. He hugged his wife tenderly while she related a shortened version of what had transpired. They soon left for hospital arm in arm and both sniffling.

The news of the accident of the four facilitators traveled through the prison like the flu. Brooksie telephoned the Warden to let her know everyone was okay. Dr. James stated she was meeting with the detectives in the next hour or so, to formulate a plan of sorts.

Rachael, Anita and Brooksie made their own plans to get together at Lucinda's house tomorrow. They wanted to process their feelings and make some decisions about the workshop. A message was left on Lucinda's phone telling her and Tony that the team would meet at their house at 10 a.m., if that would be convenient for them. If not, call them back and re-set the time.

The three, looking disheveled, worse for wear, said their good-byes and said they would meet up tomorrow at Lucinda's house. Rachael dropped Brooksie off at a car rental garage. "Guess I better get hold of my insurance person. Sure hope the damage isn't too bad and I won't have to wait a long time for my car to be fixed. I love that car."

Rachael said, "So sorry about your car. I've got to admit I'm still shaken up somewhat. I've never been someone's target before. By the way you told the detective you had a plan when you were holding that knife. What was the plan?"

"I didn't have the foggiest idea of a plan. But, I figured the four of us would come up with something. That is right after we all peed on ourselves. Thanks for the ride. See you tomorrow my friend."

CHAPTER TWENTY-FOUR

"Trouble is only opportunity in work clothes."
Henry J. Kaiser

Thursday 10 a.m.

Lucinda met her friends at the door brandishing two black swollen eyes and a stitched and bruised nose.

"Wow! Are you in a lot of pain?" asked Anita

"No. I just look worse than I feel. The good doctor stitched me up, gave me a tetanus shot and sent me on my way," answered Lucinda.

Tony greeted his wife's friends and colleagues and ushered them into the kitchen where he had been busy making coffee and baking a delicious coffee cake for them. He put out cups, plates and a appetizing bowl of fresh cut up fruit, covered lightly with honey.

"There's plenty of coffee and hot water for tea. I'll leave you ladies to whatever you need to discuss. I'll be working in the garage Lucy, call me if you need anything." He gave his new bride of less than one year, a tender kiss over her slightly swollen cheek.

She thanked him with loving look. After he was out of earshot she said, "He is an absolute treasure. I have to pinch myself to realize how lucky I am to have such a great guy plus his daughter, Katrina. She is so precious and seems to really like me and I have found it so easy to love her. Tony is very concerned for our safety. He would never try to tell me what to do, but he did say he wants us to make different plans for transportation to and from the prison. I agree with him. Any ideas?"

"Luke said the same thing to me about traveling," added Brooksie. He has offered to drive us, Lucy and myself, to and from Lancer's for the remainder of the workshops.

"Since I couldn't sleep last night I kept thinking how to keep us safe and how to keep the workshops on schedule. I don't know if you and Anita have someone that could safely transport you both to and from home or the clinic. In case you don't, I am thinking maybe we could all finish the five workshops together. We could all drive together with Tony one time and the next time with Luke. We could hold both workshops in the cafeteria like usual except we would be at opposite ends. What do you all think?"

Lucinda spoke first, "I know Tony would be happy to share the driving duties with Luke. They would only have to make the trip once a month for the next five months. Why don't I get Tony back here and ask him for his opinion?"

Anita offered to go and get him. Minutes later, Tony, walked in with a big smile, and Lucinda motioned for him to take a seat next to her.

"We have a question to ask you. No pressure. We just want your honest opinion." said Brooksie. "First off, we would like to thank you for your generous offer to drive us to Lancers. I believe my friend Luke, would also be willing to do the same. If all four of us hold our workshops on the same Wednesday every other week, then you would only need to drive the team one time a month and Luke could take us the other time. We have five workshops left to do so that makes five trips for you and five for Luke.

"Before you answer, you probably want to talk it over with Lucy and I need to ask Luke what he thinks of our proposal."

Tony took Lucy's hand in his. He looked at each upturned face of their friends and said, "I don't need time to think about it, I think it is a great solution. It's a definite 'yes', I want to be the driver of four beautiful and gifted women. But, 'yes' Brooksie, you might want to give Luke a chance to decide for himself. If he is unable to drive, I will gladly drive two times a month. It would be my pleasure."

"You're right Tony, and I will see Luke tonight and share what we have proposed to you. How about you and Lucy come to dinner at my house Friday night? That'll give me time to ask Luke and time for him to think about it. There is more safety in numbers and all of us coming together will probably please the Warden, the detectives and Sharon. I don't foresee any problems combining our two groups. We'll be far enough apart in that large mess hall so conversations will remain private and Sharon can go back and forth to each group."

Back at Lancer's Prison..........

The Warden and the detectives have met discussing the safety issues for the four facilitators. The Warden was summoned called to the phone and coincidently it was Brooksie on the other end. She shared their idea of combining the workshops on the same Wednesday, every other week, and the four would be driven to and from the prison by the husband of one and the friend of the other. The Warden instantly liked the plan and after getting off the phone she shared it with the detectives. They all agreed to the new mode of transportation and new schedule. They were also impressed by the wisdom it took, to implement such a plan.

Detective Yomoto informed the Warden that the investigation of the accident was coming together nicely. He said, we have a probable suspect. All we need is a few more pieces of the puzzle before we show our hand.

CHAPTER TWENTY-FIVE

**"Love is the only thing that can be divided
without being diminished."**
Anonymous

"Welcome Luke," Brooksie greeted him with a smile and peck on the cheek. "Thanks for coming with such short notice. I would have asked you to bring Drake, but I wasn't sure we could talk openly with him around. I'll make a special meal just for Drake, next time. Maybe even a picnic. I know he loves picnics."

"Don't worry about Drake 'cause my folks love to have him most anytime. They spoil him like crazy and he loves it. What can I do to be of help? I'm excited to be of service to you. Anything, just name it.

"Will you please carry this tray of appetizers outside in the patio? It's such a nice evening I thought we would eat on the patio and enjoy the weather. Would you mind being in charge of cooking the steelhead over the fire pit along with the corn?"

"Leave it to me. I'm a pro when it come to cooking over a fire pit. I'm always looking for ways to impress you with my handyman skills or any other kinds of skills," he shows her his best devious grin.

"Luke, I'm already impressed by your many skills," she turns quickly away before her cheeks turn the color of a tomato. *I'm*

*turning into an adolescent any time I think he is flirting with me.
I'm hopeless.*

The front door bell rings. Brooksie yells out, along with the
choir of dogs barking and Sam, the cat, meowing. Tony and
Lucinda are welcomed in by the usual dog sniffing, or also known
as the butt salute, tails wagging and eyes begging to be petted.

Lucinda hands her host a gift. "We brought a decadent dessert
created by my favorite baker, Tony of course. He made this
amaretto cheesecake this morning. If he keeps up this fantastic
cooking and baking I'll need a forklift to get me into bed." The
girls hug hello and the guys shake hands.

"Margueritas, chips and fresh salsa are waiting for us on the
patio. They settle in with the drinks and Luke begins right in
with his offer. "I can take the Wednesday next week and drive the
women to Lancers and back unless you want the first time, Tony?

After struggling to swallow a mouthful of chips and salsa,
Tony responded, That's fine with me and I'll take the next trip
two weeks later. I plan to take a different route, as recommended
by the detectives."

"And I'll do the same," answered Luke. "I'm not going to
drive them to the clinic right after we arrive back in town from
the prison. There are several interesting places to eat along the
way. One place even has a fine looking nursery with a decorating
store attached. If the ladies want, I can stop there several times
and we can have lunch and shop around. I believe it will confuse
anyone that was counting on us following some scripted routine."

"Sounds wonderful, Luke," said Lucinda."I can hardly wait to
visit that store and nursery. Good thing you have a big car. This
is wonderful of both of you to become our private transportation
service. I feel safer and will definitely sleep better at night."

Brooksie offered her deep felt thanks as well. After coffee and
another slice of Tony's terrific cheesecake, Lucy said, "It's time to

go and pick up Tony's daughter, Katrina from his deceased wife's parents house. "She loves to spend time with her grandparents, they spoil her like crazy. I believe they miss their daughter and greatly appreciate being in her daughter's life." Luke added that his son also loved being spoiled by his parents. The friends said their good-byes and Luke returned to the living room and sat down on the couch.

"Brooksie, please come and join me." She sat next to him. He took her hands in his and looked deeply into her brown eyes. "You have become so important to me. I've known for many months that I love you. The attempt on your life has made me realize just how much I want us to be a part of each other's lives. You and Drake are my family. I know we have known each other a month short of a year, but I know what I want and hope you feel the same way."

Tears started trickling down Brooksie's cheeks. She didn't release her hands in order to wipe her face. "I love you, too. I wasn't sure how you felt about me, about us."

"So will you walk down the aisle with me sometime soon?" Luke brought out a small package from his jacket and handed it to her. Her tears continued their slow descent as her hands were shaking. She opened the small box and stared at a beautiful opal and diamond ring.

"Would you stay with me tonight?" asked Brooksie. "My heart is pounding so loud, can you hear it?"

"Can't hear it, but I can feel my own speeding up. It will be my pleasure to stay and I do mean my pleasure." He smiled his sexy, dimpled grin and off to the bedroom they raced. Pets rushed right behind them all yipping in chorus with tails frantically flailing in the air. To the animals shock, the bedroom door closed and they found themselves on the other side of the door. Surely there had been a mistake made. They all sat themselves down to wait for the door to open, but eventually they all fell asleep, unlike their people companions.

CHAPTER TWENTY-SIX

**"There is nothing wrong with making mistakes.
Just don't respond with encores."**
Anonymous

Police investigators were sent out to auto repair shops in the area. They were looking for a yellow truck with damage to the front bumper. At Joe's shop, the two policeman spoke with the owner, Joe. He told them he had worked on a yellow truck yesterday. He added that there was some silver paint embedded in the bumper and the truck had broken headlight.

Joe told the officers, "I asked the owner what happened and he said he hit a deer. Then I pointed out to him the silver paint on his bumper and he stammered something about a post he hit a while back. I ordered him a new bumper and told him it would take a week or two before delivery. I also fixed his broken headlight. He paid with a Visa card. He was kinda jumpy."

"Could we please look at the receipt?" asked the officer.

Joe went into his office. He returned shortly with a copy of the receipt. "I need to keep the original for my records, if that's okay."

"That's fine. Thanks for your help," replied the officer. He glanced at the receipt and saw that it was signed by Bo Smithers. As they got back into their patrol car, he turned to his partner and said, "Detective Yomoto is going to be pleased with the signature."

Back at the precinct, Detective Yomoto had looked at the receipt and said, "I think it's time to make a visit to Mr. Smithers as soon as the background report comes in. Should be any minute now."

Detective Rowe brought the report to her partner's desk and read the summarized sheet, "Looks like three assault charges over the past ten years. He also spent one year incarcerated for the first assault and the last two were dismissed for insufficient evidence."

Detective Yomoto stood up from his uncomfortable looking chair and stated, "I think it is time to make an unannounced visit to Mr. Smithers."

The Smithers home...............

After the detectives rang the door bell numerous times and then knocked loudly on the door, Mr. Smithers finally answered the door.

"What do you people want?" growled the person who opened the door.

"Are you Mr. Bo Smithers?" asked Detective Yomoto.

"Yes I am. Is there something wrong? Let me get my wife."

At that moment Malina, the Warden's assistant, walked up and politely asked, "What can we do to help you officers?"

"We have some questions for your husband and wonder if he has a moment for us."

"What sort of questions?" she asked. "Please come in. You don't need to stand outside. Come and sit down in the kitchen. Would you would like some coffee?"

The detectives came in as they were invited to. Detective Rowe showed Mr. Smithers, the receipt. It was quickly snatched up by Malina. She looked at the paper and gave her husband an angry stare. Her pupils barely visible through the slit of her eyelids.

"It seems your truck was in an accident the other day and incurred a damaged bumper and headlight. There was evidence of silver paint on your bumper which matches the paint on the damaged car. Four social workers returning from a workshop at Lancer's Prison were intentionally hit by a truck matching your description. You can see for yourself it appears to be your signature okaying the work done by Joe's Auto Repair Shop. Can you explain this?" asked Detective Yomoto.

Bo's face turned pale and he jumped up from his chair while both detectives took defensive stances. Detective Yomoto stood up in front of Bo and announced "I am placing you under arrest for a hit and run accident" He then read Bo the Miranda Rights."

"What have you done you big, dumb ox?" screamed Mrs. Smithers. "Don't say another word until I get you a lawyer. I'm sure there is a logical explanation for the damage to his truck, but first I will get hold of our lawyer. Where will you take him?"

"To our precinct, on Rose Street. We'll be waiting there for his lawyer to show up. Do you need the address?" asked Detective Rowe.

"No I'm well aware of your location. I'm sure this will all be straightened out today or tomorrow. Remember, Bo, to talk only with Mr. Felder. He is our attorney. Okay?"

Bo was handcuffed. He offered no resistance, just looked blankly at his wife and whispered. "Why?"

As soon as her husband was taken away, in the police car, Malina called Dr. Ronan's cell phone. He answered after the third ring. "Is this important? I'm with a patient at the moment."

"Hell yes, this is important! You'd better be wearing your pants. We need to meet as soon as you get finished with your last patient. The shit may be hitting the fan. Bo has just been arrested. Meet me at the same place 6:30 p.m. after you give your report to Dr. Gibran, unless you think you can get away sooner."

"Okay I'll be there," responded the doctor.

Later.............
Malina meets up with the doctor. He reaches out for her and she nearly trips over her own feet trying to get away from his grasp.

"What's the matter with you Malina? I only wanted to hug you. It's been so long since I've even touched you."

"Mitch, I don't think you understand just how serious this situation has become. Bo, the moron, is sitting in jail at this very moment. He has a smaller brain than my cat and will tell all to the police. You need to put together a file on him, dated one or two years back. You need to paint a picture of him having blackouts, a history of steroid use, and episodes of violent behaviors toward me. It would be best if you could get your psychiatrist friend, Dr. Jensen, to collaborate your suspicions of Bo. He has a history of ongoing drug use and mental illness. That report will probably cost you a pretty penny, but Bo could mess up your finances by interfering with your successful drug business."

"Me, why do I have to pay? I don't want to ask Jensen to falsify records. He'll want a bigger percentage of what I collect. He's a greedy son-of-a bitch and I've never trusted him. I'm not made of money. Anyway, my wife has been asking questions lately about our accounts. She is not stupid when it comes to our finances."

"She's stupid enough. You been screwing around for years and she has no clue."

"Let's not go there again. For Christ's sake, what are we going to do?" A small amount of drool slithers down of the sides of his mouth as his face and ear lobes are flushed red.

"I feel sick to my stomach," complained the doctor. "We are in this together. Tell me, what can we do?"

"I told you," screeched Malina. "You refer Bo to a psychiatrist. Make up a chart on Bo showing his diminishing mental state and act like your usual charming self, especially towards your dreamy eyed nurse."

Mitchell lowers his head, covers his face with his large, shaking, well- manicured hands and cries out, " What is going to happen to us?" Tears began making their way down his unshaven face.

"Get a grip! I've told you exactly what you're going to do. If you want the same cushy life, get a hold of yourself and do as I say." She caresses his arm and rubs his neck and seductively places her hands on his knees and slowly massages his thighs. "Things will work out. Let's get together next week, way out of town. In fact I'll make reservations at Sea Point Inn for Sunday night. We need some comfort time, don't you think? Tell your wife there is a doctor's convention. There is always some sort of convention going on near that hotel."

CHAPTER TWENTY-SEVEN

"To start to become aware of the ways in which our responses to loss have shaped us can be the beginning of wisdom."
Judith Viorst.....*Necessary Losses*

"Ladies all aboard for the eight glorious programs at Lancers," bellowed Tony. "I'm honored to be your driver and protector on this my first time to transport you beauties. Buckle up and enjoy the ride."

"He has been so excited about this ever since we made the plan to combine our workshops. It took him twenty minutes to decide what to wear on this maiden voyage," said Lucinda giggling. She sat in front with her husband while the others took the back seats.

"I'm feeling so much better about Tony and Luke driving us. I didn't want to be such a coward, but I have really been scared," shared Anita.

All agreed to feeling much safer now and better able to focus on their group of inmates and their needs. The drive time seemed to go by quickly and soon they were pulling into the prison's parking lot. It had been decided earlier that Tony would wait at the coffee shop that was located about twenty minutes from Lancer's. He brought a book and some paper work with him. He left for his destination and said he would be waiting for them at 11:30 or whenever they came out through the gate.

Workshop #8...............

Sharon walked into the mess hall accompanied by two new COs, one male and one female. She had been released from the hospital the day before. Her left arm was in a cast and she had numerous fading bruises were visible on her neck and face. Her face was still slightly swollen especially, around her eyes and around a long line of stitches, that went from her nose across her cheek, stopping at the jaw line. They snaked along like a twisting river.

A cheer arose from the small workshop groups when they saw her. She smiled a crooked smile, due to the path of the laceration. Several inmates patted her gently on the back and offered their heartfelt encouragement.

"Welcome back Sharon. You have been sorely missed." said Brooksie.

Sharon acknowledged the warm greetings. "Glad to be out of the hospital, but can't say I'm thrilled to be back in Lancers." She addressed the inmates, "As you can all see we have had to bring the two groups together on the same day. One group will please move over to the far end of the cafeteria that way one group will not hear what they other group is discussing or sharing. We had to combine all of you in order to keep the four facilitators safe. I know you probably all heard the news about the attempt on their lives last Wednesday. They now ride together with a male driver for protection. I'm so grateful they continue to believe in the importance of these workshops that they are even willing to place themselves in danger.

"So if Brooksie's and Lucinda's group will remain here, Rachael's and Anita's group will move to the other side, we can begin our eight workshop."

Once everyone was settled, Lucinda began, "Today's workshop will be about grief, loss and respectful communication. Think about how you handle your sadness, anger, anguish, fear and confusion when you experience loss. Any and all kinds of loss."

It was the consensus of the inmates that getting away from all painful feelings as fast as possible, was the number one priority. Some used drugs, alcohol or a combination of both. Others overate, mostly on junk foods. Some started fights with anyone they could aggravate or bully. They all agreed they acted in hateful and hostile ways. Destructive behaviors were the most common reactions to emotional pain due to losses.

"I usually remain calm and plan my revenge," offered Delores.

Sammy spoke up, "You all know what I do, I beat the hell out of someone. My mind goes blank and I want that sick piece of crap partner of mine dead. Now I'm sorry she's paralyzed, but I'm not sorry I hurt her for what she did to my innocent pets."

Brooksie asked, "What do you wish you had done differently, if anything?"

"I'd kick her out of my house and my mind and never look back." Sammy crossed her arms and sat up straighter in her chair.

Sharon surprised the group by saying, "I'd like to share my feelings toward the two women who tried to kill me, and add my gratefulness to Houston and Wilamina. Sasha, I understand you also tried to defend me. My thanks to you as well.

"I don't know the attackers, don't know why they wanted me dead or why someone would put them up to such a crime. I'm at a loss to understand anyone who could hurt a stranger. Even though my schooling was focused on all forms of hurts from childhood and how those cruelties, traumas and tragedies affected the growing up adult, I still don't understand random acts of assault and murder. I know I murdered my own sister. It was the action I chose to commit for the safety of others and the kindest act I could do for the sister I loved. It seems to me that when we feel helpless and have come from an unloving, traumatic background, the worst feeling is that of helplessness.

"My emotions are up and down like a roller coaster. Through trial and error, I have discovered that I can lessen my anger and anxiety when I exercise, write new workshops, or talk to good listeners about my feelings and then I just give myself permission to feel my anger, rage and fear regarding the two paid assassins. I think about the three women who saved my life. I've decided to take the self-defense class, offered here, to deal more effectively with my fear of possible future attacks. I'm reading some books having to do with death and dying in order to face up to my own fear of dying.

"Lastly, I remind myself frequently, I'm not to blame for the beating I took, the attackers are responsible. I'm responsible for my own reactions and behaviors. They can go to hell for all I care. I have a life to live and by God I'm going to do the best I can wherever I find myself, even here in Lancers."

"So we are all kind of alike with the same feelings?" questioned Wilamina thoughtfully. "When I find I'm in a shit-hole it's okay to feel shitty, but it's up to me to climb out and not beat the shit out of others. When someone is ragging on my friends or on me I just have to stop them anyway I can."

Brooksie waited to see if Sharon was going to respond. Sharon pointed at at Brooksie to let her know she could answer Willy.

"Wilamina, there is a difference when someone is just ragging on you and when you or your friends are actually in danger of physical harm. You saved your brother's life. I believe that was the right choice. Houston saved her mother's life again a right choice. You both saved Sharon's life. The question to ask is, did you continue to beat the attackers long after they were no longer a threat? I'm talking about controlling feelings of anger, hate and so forth. Taking control of a bad situation and then controlling your own emotions is not easy, but definitely necessary. I remember watching two male dogs squaring off once. Dominance was the trigger. They fought loud and hard for a minute, then one got hurt and rolled over and whimpered. The other dog stood over him for a second and then walked away. He knew he was the male in charge and that was all he needed to show.

"The feeling of helplessness can be terrifying. There are many responses to that feeling. Getting drunk, drugged, overeating, suicide, violence, having multiple sex partners, nasty behaviors, cruelty, sarcasm, bullying, stealing, lying, and on and on. The greatest loss is loss of your own belief in yourself. You don't believe you have an important role, an important place on this planet, town, street or family. You have lost faith in your own ability and potential."

"I have believed for so long, since my baby died, when I was sixteen, that I was devil bad. I was helpless, had no hope of ever doing anything right again. If my family, the church and Jose's family knew I was going to hell, why would I think I was worth anything. No one thought I was worth talking to. But, I found a lot of people who thought I was worth screwing. How do I start to believe I am worth something good? I'm not something to throw away." Corrina put her hands over her face and bent over the table, sobbing.

Wilamina and Lucinda both moved quickly over to where Corrina was and put their arms around her. "Oh Cory, I'm so sorry about your stinkin' family. They was wrong. They was mean and crazy, " choked out Willy. Lucinda's face all wet and blotchy as she gently patted Corrina's back.

After a time the discussion continued to be animated and intense. There were a few civil arguments about the right and wrong of payback. Berri's voice could be heard over the rest. "I'm never going to be through with my anger and missing my Ali every day. I'm not sorry Sam is dead. I'm just sorry his mama didn't drown him when he was a baby. The courts and them lawyers was never gonna do right by Ali. Sam always got away with his shit. He'd sit in jail for a while and then like always, he was out on the street to do more shit."

"I've never had a child so I've never lost one," remarked Sasha. "So I have no idea what that feels like, Berri. But, my mom had her first baby die, she was my sister. She was only one year old and my mother never recovered from her grief. I swear she cried for one year straight, and then hit the bottle with a vengence. My dad tried all kinds of way to help her, but she simply refused to let anyone help her. Broke my dad's heart and left me feeling unwanted. Her liver finally gave out, because of too much booze. Maybe if she had talked about her feelings she might have made it. Didn't mean to go on and on Berri, just saying maybe if you talked more about how you're feeling, you'd get some relief. Hell, what do I know."

Brooksie affirmed Sasha's idea of letting out her feelings that it might offer some relief and peace. "Like a teapot sitting over a hot burner. When the water reaches a boil it lets of steam. If the teapot is unable to let off the steam the pot will simply burn it's bottom up and become useless."

Berri responded, "I already have a black ass, guess I can't be burned anymore." Her nostrils flared and she glanced briefly at the faces around the table. "Anyone here ever have their baby murdered and die in pain?" Silence followed. "I didn't think so.

Don't try to tell me about the pain of loss. I'm dying inside and I can't stand it."

"You're absolutely right Berri, none of us can feel your pain or anger. I'm not saying I know how you feel and I don't believe anyone here thinks they can exactly feel like you do, but we can all feel pain, sorrow, and compassion for you, one human for another. It is true, you are alone with your feelings, but it is also true that sharing pain does eventually take some of the sting away, lessens the sense that you are completely alone in your suffering," responded Brooksie.

Berri opened and closed her mouth, like she was struggling to find the right words. "I'm sorry I can't stop hating. It's eaten me up inside. I know you and others want me to feel differently, but I can't. I would want to kill Sam all over again if I could."

Lucinda looked kindly at Berri and said, "We are not wanting you to feel differently than you do, Brooksie was simply talking about sharing the feelings you have. They are your feelings for the terrible thing that was done to precious Ali. We can have compassion for another and feel pain, helplessness and sorrow for another's deep anguish. I have my own feelings about your feelings."

"I'm not so good with words like most of you, but I can say I'm a mother, a bad one so far. I do have my own feelings about how I didn't do right by my girls and those feelings hurt me, makes me ashamed of myself," shared Luella. "It's my fault if I lose them and just thinkin' this makes me real sad and real guilty. I'm to blame, but Berri you are not to blame for Ali's death, Sam is. You was having to go to work to feed your baby 'cause you loved him. I worked some just to buy more dope. I didn't ever think about my babies and only thought about dope."

"Thanks for trying to make me feel better, Lu. Maybe this talking ain't so bad after all," remarked Berri.

CHAPTER TWENTY-EIGHT

**"I've learned.....That no matter
how serious your life
required you to be, everyone needs
a friend to act goofy with."**
Andy Rooney

Facilitators lunch date.....

Brooksie could hardly wait to meet her friends for lunch. She couldn't keep her eyes off her beautiful engagement ring. She hoped she could control herself and not blurt out what a loving, generous lover Luke turned out to be. *I've never been so sure of anything in my life as I am that Luke and I are truly good together, maybe even perfect for each other. I can be myself, so can he. He really likes me and encourages me to have goals, and wants to help me reach them. I feel the same for him. I know there will be bumps in the road, but at least we will hold hands as we go over them. Marino wanted me to be a certain way. He made me feel like I was only okay if I stayed in place. Luke is happy for me to soar and I want the same for him. My God how did I get so damn fortunate.*

The team had all arrived early at the Table Talk Cafe. Apparently all anxious to vent and share concerns.

"God, I'm glad we have these lunches to let off steam," blurted out Lucinda. "Sometimes I feel like a tea pot sitting over a hot flame and unable to open my spout and release the steam."

"Great analogy," replied Rachael. "I'm walking daily, faster and faster for four or so miles and it seems to be helping me relieve my anxiety. At this rate I'm going to be a skinny minny and can quit my current profession and become one of those super skinny models."

Anita chimed in, "How does your lawyer friend feel about a super thin girlfriend?"

"Anita, I told you we are just friends."

The others rolled their eyes, snickered and gave Rachael 'that look' of 'oh really'.

Brooksie said, "If you girls don't mind I'd like to say that I love having both groups at the same time, for a number of reasons. One reason is that we have more time to visit driving to and from the prison. The other reason is that we, get to know two men better and have a little fun and diversion after our Wednesday workshop." She repeatedly used her left hand to push away an imaginary hair from her forehead. She did it several times without her friends noticing anything. She slipped her left hand under the table and rested it on her lap. *I'm not sure when to tell them my great news. Sometimes I feel so damn insecure or maybe bit immature.*

"I agree wholeheartedly, "concurred Anita. The two others also were in agreement.

"We must remember what the detectives warned us about even when we are not together. We should pay attention to our surroundings, notice if we are being followed, or if we have an uneasy feeling. We need to keep our houses locked up tight and avoid being out alone after dark. Sounds like wise advice to me. I'm taking their suggestions to heart. I just don't want to become paranoid and start acting crazy," revealed Brooksie."

She continued. "Recently I remembered something that I started to think about in the middle of the night. After a workshop session, Delores asked me how far was it to the grief clinic and what route was the best one to take. Said she had a friend who lived near Lancer's and may be interested in attending a divorce group. I didn't think anything of it at the time, but we were attacked soon after her inquiry. Could be just an honest question, on her part, but my suspicions now are aroused."

Anita offered her opinion. She thought it would be a good idea to share Delores's question with the detectives and the Warden.

"You never mentioned that to me," said Lucinda.

"I just thought about it again last night. I don't want us to get more anxious,but I also don't want to miss something that could be important. I'll mention it to the Warden and the detectives next time we meet."

Lucinda asked the group, "Do anyone of you think the police are getting any closer to finding out who killed Simone, who attacked Sharon and who tried to hurt us?"

Anita said that she had no idea.

Brooksie responded, "I feel like they know a great deal more than they have told us. I do believe they are hard at work on the investigation. I have the feeling they are close to making some arrests. Our job is to stay focused on Sharon's great program."

"Rachael, did you hear anything from Mr. Lagunta about Houston and Wilamina?"

"I believe he is working on getting both of them a new trial or whatever," said Rachael. "He is also working for one of the inmates in our group. I know nothing about the time frame for the three. I do know he has his staff working many hours for them. I don't ask him much because of confidentiality issues and he doesn't ask about the inmates and the sessions for the same reason. I do believe he is dedicated to justice. He is a good man."

"And you are a very good woman," added Brooksie

Brooksie had purposely kept her left hand under the table throughout the conversations, but then slowly slipped her hand up and used her left hand with her new ring, to pick up her coffee cup. She conspicuously ran her cup by each of her friends faces. Lucinda spotted the ring almost immediately and blurted out, "You're engaged! I knew he was the one." She jumped out of her chair and grabbed Brooksie for a big bear hug. Anita teared up and offered her heartfelt congratulations. Rachael took Brooksie's hand, squeezed it and said, "My dear friend, I'm so happy for the two of you. You are a great team and may you grow closer every year."

"I believe the four of us have four good men in our lives. I can't say enough about Luke's kindness, thoughtfulness and his playfulness. He is so much fun to be around and we laugh a lot. When the 'doubting Thomas' side of me emerges, I think about my weak spots, but Luke doesn't seem to have any. Then I find myself stupidly thinking that he is too good for me and if he really knew me, he'd quickly run in the other direction. I know you are all my dear friends and will probably try to reassure me of my worthiness, but I have to deal with my feelings about myself and get past my own obstacles."

Rachael asked, "Can you share the reasons you feel less deserving of this great relationship?"

"I worry he won't find me interesting in the long run. I worry I won't be a good mom to Drake. I like, actually, I need time alone. I like sitting in my garden surrounded by my pets and not having to do anything but smell the flowers and pet the pets. Maybe I'm too selfish to be a wife."

"I can understand that," said Anita. "I not only want to be alone often, but I too need time away from people in general. I'm de-energized by crowds and sometimes even four or more people make me feel uncomfortable and cranky."

"I didn't realize that about you, Anita and I feel the same way often. I get energy from alone time and from others. I guess I'm more of an introvert than an extrovert. How does the role of a full-time wife and mother fit this picture?" asked Brooksie.

Rachael spoke up, "I think we become better people when we honor our true needs. Most of us seem to fall in the middle of being both introverted and extroverted. A wise person, will find their own niche, through trial and error. Maybe you could share your concerns with Luke. He might surprise you with his response."

"I will try and do that Rachael. And thank you all for your friendship and caring advice. This Sunday, Luke is going with me to Aunt Tilly's and Uncle Joe's to delight them with our news. My Aunt has been conniving for several years to get me hitched. Now I suppose Luke and I will have several new pets with ribbons around their necks to show they are wedding gifts. She and Uncle Joe are treasures. They have stood behind me, with gentle encouragement and sometimes a little push. And throughout my teenage destructive years they have continued to be in my corner. If the inmates only had people like my aunt and uncle in their lives, their futures could have been so different. I truly believe it only takes one adult to love, nurture and never give up on us to make our lives so much more productive and joyful. Sorry, it seems I've jumped on the band wagon. I'm just overwhelmed with how fortunate I am. If it hadn't been for my aunt and uncle, maybe I would be where many of these women are today-behind bars."

Rachael asked, "And what sort of crime do you think you might have committed in order to become an inmate?"

Brooksie thought for a minute, "I might have murdered someone. There were a few despicable people in my life. Aunt Tilly taught me how to handle my anger and hate with directness. She also taught me the importance of laughter. Uncle Joe showed me the power of prioritizing and patience. What crimes would any of you have considered committing?" directing her eyes around the table.

"That's easy for me to answer," said Rachael. "I'd be arrested for stealing food, clothes and probably money. I was damn poor when I was very young and I can remember actually being hungry a few times. I don't think I could have stood to have a hungry, cold baby or child. I really believe I would have stolen whatever my baby needed."

"I must admit, sometimes I thought of putting something in my mother's coffee to make her go to sleep permanently," shared Lucinda. "So my crime would have been murder. Thank God I didn't do anything, but I did entertain the idea at times when she was driving me crazy. Thanks to all of you and Tony, I choose to simply remove the toxic person from my life."

Anita said, "I'm trying hard to think of what crime I would've committed. My step-mother was the worst person I've ever had to deal with on a regular basis. Can't say I wanted to kill her, but I can say I hoped she would've drop dead, in front of me and my brother when she was being so mean. I'm such a wimp. I don't think I would do very well as an inmate." She started to giggle and the others joined in the merriment.

"I read this quote in a book long ago," shared Brooksie. "It said, 'Laughter is a tranquilizer with no side effects.' written by Arnold Glasow. It's one of the few quotes I remember."

The friends continued to share for another hour and eventually felt talked out. They agreed to be watchful, lock all doors and do what the detectives recommended.

CHAPTER TWENTY-NINE

**"You will not be punished for your anger,
you will be punished by your anger."**
Gautama Buddha (563-483 BC)

Workshop #9

"This topic may stand your hairs on end, but give yourself time to look at forgiveness as a way to help yourself," suggested Brooksie. "Speaking strictly for myself, forgiving myself for making numerous bad choices has been harder than forgiving others for hurting me."

"I'm the same way," agreed Lucinda. "It has taken me years to forgive myself for thinking so poorly of my own mother. She was and still is a terrible mother. She never thought of me as a unique, lovable or worthwhile child or even as a adult. In her eyes, I was only alive to satisfy her self-centered needs. It has been a real trial for me to forgive myself for not loving her. I believed in my soul I was a bad person for my hateful feelings towards my own flesh and blood. Finally, I realized why wouldn't I hate a person who treated me so poorly. So I simply gave myself permission to feel and admit I hated her. What happened next was quite a surprise. It didn't take long, but my deep feelings of anger towards my mother slowly turned into pity and sadness for her and all that she missed out on enjoying a great kid, me. I realized she was the one who lost out, not me. I've been free of her for a long time now and have discovered I've forgiven myself for my negative and destructive feelings towards someone who missed out on the joy of parenthood. I'm loving the role of being a stepmom. My mother just never got it, and she has become the loser.

"Sorry I didn't mean to go on and on, but this subject has meant so much in my life," added Lucinda.

"Sammy, may I use you as an example?" asked Brooksie.

"Yeah, sure," returned Sammy.

"If you can honestly forgive yourself for leaving your dogs alone with your mentally ill partner, you'll be a winner. You never would have put your dogs in harm's way if you had believed she would do the unthinkable. It was her responsibility to take her medication. She was an adult and you were neither her doctor nor policeman. Your understanding of her mental condition and the drugs prescribed for her disorder were not a part of your education. If you had known more and had a crystal ball you would have done differently, true?"

"Yes ma'am. I surely would've."

Brooksie continued, "I'm not suggesting you forget your strong feelings about the perpetrators of cruelty, but it's important to do something to stop cruelty when you encounter it. Holding on to the hate and anger only hurts you, not the perpetrators.

"The whole point of forgiveness is to move on and do better. If we repeatedly beat ourselves over the head for harmful actions, then we stay stuck. We stay addicted. We stay mean and we stay rooted in the same quick sand of bitterness."

"I'll never forgive Sam for killing my baby. And I can never forgive myself for leaving him with that piece of shit," blasted Berri.

"That is your choice, Berri. I will never forget that your sweet baby was murdered by Sam and I will never forget that you were not responsible. I cannot imagine losing a baby, but my heart aches for you and the unspeakable loss of your son," affirmed Lucinda.

"Berri, you're still alive. Maybe you can help others who have had to bury their beloved children. Your life's not over and Ali still lives in your heart. Maybe it would make Ali happy if his mama was helping other poor souls who lost their precious babies. Every night I say a prayer to Jesus for Ali and you," exclaimed Wilamina.

"Mr. Blackmore says no one over eighteen is completely blameless. He says making mistakes is how we learn and develop character," offered Sammy timidly.

Houston added, "He sounds like a good man to work for and to know, Sammy."

"We are going to take a ten minute break and let you think about who or what you might need to forgive yourself for. I'll leave the index cards and pencils here if you want to write down some of your ideas," advised Brooksie.

While the inmates were busy with the assignment, Sharon and the two facilitators moved over to another table. "Sharon you look good. How are you really feeling?" inquired Lucinda.

"I'm doing very well. I'm so grateful for the workable change you all came up with. This combining workshop days is a fantastic idea and thank God, Tony and Luke are providing the taxi service. I was nearly crazy with fear for all of you."

"Same goes for you. We were all losing sleep over our concerns for your safety. I take it those two CO's sitting over there against the wall are your bodyguards?" inquired Brooksie.

"I'm glad they're around, but it's like having a shadow, kind of creepy, especially at night. Houston and Willy both hover over me like helicopters. Thanks again for coming up with this great plan to combine the workshop days. I'm going to meander over to Rachael and Anita's group. I love this arrangement. See you guys later. Thanks again."

The short break was over and Brooksie asked, "Wilamina, what about what you did to your boyfriend who nearly killed your brother, Royal? What are the feelings left over from that day, if any?"

"Shamed to say this, but my boyfriend was a cheating piece of shit. Don't know what I was thinkin' gettin' mixed up with such trash. My brother finally had gotten away from the dope, and dirt bag wanted him to get out and sell for him. Royal refused, so they started yelling at each other, louder and louder. My brother's not a real big guy. The meth he was on took away his appetite. He'd gotten skinny over the years, lost most of his muscle. Anyway, Armon was strong like a bull. When he'd get into a fight he'd get mean. He worked out. He was too smart to take any of the drugs he was selling, so he took pretty good care of himself. He was in much better shape than Royal, so when he started to punch him, it didn't take long for Royal to be in trouble. Even when my brother was down on the ground, Armon kept kicking and punching him. I went crazy. First I hit him with an ash tray, then with my fists, then my feet and I couldn't stop. I remember he had a knife. He stuck me in the leg and he was crawling over toward my brother, holding the bloody knife. That's when I hit him again as hard as I could. He fell backwards and I guess he hit his head on the stove. I'm glad I saved Royal's life. He is doing real good. He has a decent job and no drugs. He has a real nice girlfriend and baby. I'm not sorry I went after Armon, but I'm sorry he died. He was a no good nigger. I only wanted him to stop hurting Royal. I think he went crazy and wasn't going to stop until my brother was dead. I feel sad and mad I ever liked him. What kinda person does that make me? Forgiveness? That's for Jesus and I gotta trust Jesus forgives me, amen."

The group remained speechless for a few minutes. Corrina broke the silence, "You did the right thing, Willy. Jesus knows your heart and you are for sure forgiven. Do you forgive yourself?"

"I leave that to the Man upstairs. I'm moving on and soon I'll be working and helping some folks and singing. My soul can sing. I got me a business partner, a brother and sister-in-law and a baby niece. Got some good friends and a fine lawyer. I'm good."

"I'm not a good person, like Willy. If I start to think of Jose, the church, my family and his family I get all stirred up inside. I used to pray down on my knees. Look what it got me. Two dead babies and Jose and everyone else blamed me for their deaths and everything else that went wrong. How do you forgive such horrible people who convince you that you would be better off dead or should have never been born? I believed them and I guess I still do, at times. At least not all the time now."

Houston said, "Corrina, I don't know a whole lot about much, but I do know that your cruel, ignorant relatives, and the others you mentioned, were simply cowards. They didn't have the guts to look inside themselves to see the worms crawling around in their hearts. They couldn't admit their failures or weakenesses, so they made you the scapegoat. They are nothing but lying cowards. You were their punching bag. Now you have the chance to make whatever you want of yourself right here at Lancer's. Someday you're going to make a name for yourself by helping all kinds of kids. Like Mother Theresa, you love the little ones. You will make a difference for them."

Sasha interjected, "She's right Corrina, you can make a real difference with kids and teenagers. You've been there, done that and that's called real experience. You can talk their talk and they will respond to a fellow traveler, someone who has walked in their shoes. Forgiveness is not so hard for me 'cause I recognize we are all flawed in some way. So we're all in this place together. I see judgments of myself and others as a waste of time. My motto is: If I never quit, I can't fail."

"That's a great motto to live by. Mistakes are how we learn and forgiving ourselves is simply the step to take after we make a mistake. I need to learn something from my mistakes and then I can do a better job the next time," added Brooksie.

"Luella, do you have something you want to share?" asked Lucinda.

"I've really hurt my kids because of my addiction to meth and other junk. I think I could forgive myself when I'm able to make it up to them or to make it right for them. I have to stay clean, work hard with my dad and make a real home for my kids, then I will forgive myself."

"That sounds like a good plan. Did everyone share who wanted to? No one is speaking up and our time is nearly up for today. If in two weeks anyone wants to bring up their own forgiveness challenges, please do so. See you all in two weeks and keep on keeping on."

CHAPTER THIRTY

**"I've learned that we are
responsible for what we do,
no matter how we feel."**
Andy Rooney

Bo Smithers met with the lawyer his wife had quickly obtained. Malina Smithers, Mr. Felder, the attorney, and Bo were directed to an interview room at the police station. As soon as the door was closed, they seated themselves and Malina began, "Bo don't say one word until I'm finished talking."

Bo nodded. Mr. Felder opened a notebook and held his pen ready to jot down some notes.

Malina started in almost breathlessly, "Bo has been having some health problems and lately his thinking has been, let's say, confused. I've been asking him to see a mental health counselor for the past few months."

"What the hell are you talking about Malina?" bellowed Bo.

"Shut your trap you muscle bound Tarzan," screeched Malina. "I told you to let me do the talking first and you can........," Mr. Felders interrupted her and said, "Mr. Smithers, you will have your chance next. Please let your wife finish her statement. Go on Mrs. Smithers."

"As I was saying, he has been under a great deal of stress lately and he is forgetful at times. He works three different jobs while keeping up his own body building routine. I've repeatedly asked him to slow down, but to no avail. Dr. Ronan is aware of Bo's difficulties."

"Have you gone crazy? What are you talking about Malina? You're the one seeing the great doc. In fact, you see him lots of times and not only at the prison," replied Bo angrily.

"Bo, I'm trying to help you. You're in a bad situation and if you'll be quiet I can help you. Please be a good boy and let me take care of this," pleaded Malina. She stroked his head and rubbed his hand, displaying an angelic and concerned mother appearance. Her eyes dripping with concern.

Mr. Felder eventually got his questions answered, mostly by the doting wife. He went over the information about Bo driving his yellow truck and hitting the facilitator's car two times, hard enough to push them off the road and then he drove away. He continued to relay the facts so far. "The following morning Bo, you drove your truck to Joe's Auto Repair shop and let Joe order a new bumper and repair a broken head light. Joe took a colored picture of the broken head light and of your dented fender. He apparently does this routinely for the insurance claims. Do you remember driving your truck two times into the facilitator's Suburban?"

"No, of course he doesn't remember the supposed accident. He would have told me about it, if it had happened. You never said anything to me about any kind of accident." Malina looked directly at Bo with her penetrating eyes as she squeezed his hand so forcefully Bo groaned.

"No, I guess I don't remember hitting anyone. She's right I am forgetful sometimes."

Mr. Felder asked Bo, "Why did you take your truck to the repair shop?"

"Cause the damn truck was messed up. I like to keep my stuff in good shape. Is that a crime?" snapped Bo.

"Let's stop for today. I'll see Bo alone again tomorrow, I will talk with both of you again day after tomorrow. I need to speak with Dr. Ronan. I will need a signed permission from both of you to present to the doctor. Will that be a problem?" questioned the attorney.

"Of course that won't be a problem," snipped Malina. "We'll cooperate in every way."

Bo was taken by an officer back to a holding cell in the jail. He looked dazed and continued to stare at his wife as he was led away.

Malina walked out with Mr. Felder and asked him to accompany her to the cafe across the street. He first took a look at her and hesitantly agreed. Malina was thirty-three years old, 5' 9", barefooted, flaming natural red hair, a striking beauty that could have just arrived from Ireland. When they entered the cafe, she led him to a booth in a far corner. As soon as they were seated across from one another, her leg brushed his leg.

Malina acted embarrassed about her leg brushing his and said with a come-hither look, "Oh, excuse me, Mr. Felder, but I'm so distraught about Bo's condition and how the accident with his truck might look suspicious. You've got to understand about his changes in behavior. They have been coming on slowly for quite some time. Dr. Ronan will be able to shed some light for you."

"Mrs. Smithers, you are a very attractive woman and I'm not immune to a beautiful ladies' charms. If I'm to represent your husband's case, I will need to get reliable answers from several sources about his so-called physical and mental problems. You do understand don't you?"

"Yes indeed. You aren't suggesting I'm flirting with you are you?"

"Time will tell, Malina. Can I call you by your first name?" giving her a wink.

"Please do Chuck."

They left the cafe in their own cars.

CHAPTER THIRTY-ONE

The worst thing to be without.....hope.
Anonymous

Appointment day.........

Mr. Lagunta made arrangements to meet with the three inmates he had taken on pro bono, Houston, Wilamina and Susie. The three were all anxiously awaiting for their turn to speak with him and hopefully receive some good news about a retrial.

Houston was called to a small interview room first. Her mouth was horribly dry and her forehead and the palms of her hands were beginning to perspire profusely.

"Good day, Miss Houston. You look different since our last meeting. Are you sporting a new hairdo? If so, it is very flattering."

"Thank you Mr. Lagunta. I actually used the hair salon they offered here. I got a real haircut for a change. Thanks for noticing." She took a deep breath and tried to calm herself from the inside out. "I'm really nervous, sir. I'm hoping for good news, but dreading the worst," She wiped her forehead off with her sleeve. She was aware her hands were shaking and did her best to hide it from her lawyer.

"I won't keep you in suspense. We have a court date four months from now. My dedicated staff have been as busy as beavers and believe me, we will be ready to present our case on your behalf. I wanted to give you the news myself. I do have a few more questions to ask you. In the months to come, I will need to talk with you fairly often. You may get tired of the questions, especially if they are asked more than once. My assistant, Mrs. Sheila Shonte, will probably be the one who calls or visits with you. She and I will take turns gathering information from Wilamina and Susie."

They talked for fifteen more minutes, said their goodbyes, as they shook hands. Houston repeatedly thanked her lawyer. Tears formed in her eyes which she quickly brushed away.

Wilamina was next to enter the room. She flopped down into a chair and immediately began to sob. "I'm sorry, I'm so sorry, but I don't do bad news good. I saw Houston wiping her eyes when she came out of your office and she hardly never cries, so I figured bad news for her gonna mean bad news for me too."

"Whoa Miss Wilamina, tears can be shed for good news as well as bad news. I have good news for you like I did for Miss Houston. We have a trial date for you in five months from today. Now quit your crying, blow your nose and let's get to answering some questions."

Wilamina's quiet sobbing became a boisterous wail. "My God, thank you, Jesus and you, Mr. Lagunta. You mean I might really get out of here before I turn old and crabby?"

She jumped out of her chair, raced over to her wide-eye attorney. He sat frozen in front of Wilamina's wild looking arms stretched out towards him. She was a substantially built woman. She hugged him hard yelling, "Thank you, thank you. You are an angel from God."

He gently untangled her strong, fleshy arms from his body and said, "please take a seat so we can continue and I do appreciate your genuine display show of gratefulness, but our time is limited." He went on to tell her about the calls and visits from his assistant and soon their time was over. When they had finished with their questions for each other, he accompanied her to the door. He had to practically pry his hands from her warm hands. He could hear her praising Jesus, and himself as she made her way down the hall, singing Amazing Grace.

He thought to himself as he watched Wilamina walk down the hall, *I've got to get back to the gym. I was sure she could've over powered me. How embarrassing that would be.*

His last client was far more reserved when she too was told she had a court date in six months. Susie thanked her attorney politely and the two walked out together. "I hope you know how grateful I am for your help, but I'm not very demonstrative like the other two women."

Mr. Lagunta winked and smiled at her saying, "I'm more comfortable with your style and I thank you for your gratitude."

Weekend visiting time...........

Luella had a surprise visitor, her dad. He had visited last week and now here he was again. It was difficult for him to get to the prison, so he and his daughter had agreed he would visit once every other month. So here he was which delighted Luella. Her dad was wearing a thread bare suit with a freshly washed and ironed white shirt. The cuffs on the shirt were frayed. The heels of his shoes were worn down close to having no heels at all. Every so often, he would wipe away a tear and blow his nose with gusto. He nervously shifted on the bench until he was told to follow the CO to the visiting area.

His daughter, rushed over and hugged him tightly. Kissed his cheek and said, "Papa, I'm so glad you came today. You look real tired and your eyes are red."

"I have something important to tell you," whispered Mr. Garcia. "The girls are okay, better than ever. You know they have been in a foster home for close to two years now. I see them once a month at a place where the social workers watch me and them. They are both in school. They smile always and we talk both Spanish and English. They wear pretty dresses and hug their foster mom all the time."

Miss Gomez is their social worker and she checks in on them every week. Every month, she tells me how happy they are. The good foster family wants to keep them. They want to adopt them and......."

Luella shouted,, "No, no, how can you talk like this? They're your granddaughters. I thought you loved them. They belong with us." Sobbing quietly, she grabs her father's hands.

Mr. Garcia gently stroked his only daughter's hands. "It is because I love them I want them to live with this great family. We don't know when you will get out of here. I can only see them once a month. I work seven days a week for many months in the spring to fall. They are happy with those people. They take them to a Catholic church, take them to the doctors and even to a dentist. We must do the best for them to give them a chance for a good life. I can't, and you can't. We both love them. We must do what is right."

Both father and daughter held on tight to each other and cried. "They will forget us, Papa. How will they know we love them if we give them away to strangers? Maybe they will hate us. They are my reason for living, for fighting my addictions. How can you ask me this?"

"Because I love my granddaughters and I want them to have a better life. Because we both love them. They have a chance now. The social worker said she will talk with you. You can ask her all the questions you want to. Please look into your heart and ask God to help you do what is right."

"Okay Papa, I'll think about what you say and I'll talk with Miss Gomez."

They said their weepy good-byes, walked their separate ways with heads down and tears dripping onto the floor.

Later that day.....

Mr. Lagunta telephoned Rachael and informed her about the court dates for the three inmates and asked her to share the date information with Brooksie.

"Since I've got you on the phone, would you have dinner with me Saturday? I would like to take you to the ranch restaurant that your friend, Brooksie recently visited. I understand it is very casual. Tennis shoes and a light jacket are recommended. We could even pet some animals, if we're so inclined. Do you have any allergies?"

"Roco, I would love to go there! Brooksie made it sound almost magical. Of course, she is animal crazy. I'm not sure how you feel about pets and other critters. To answer your question about allergies, thank goodness I have none."

"As far as animals go, Rachael, I have two cats and they are spoiled rotten. They have me completely trained to do their bidding. I would have dogs, but I'm not home enough to care for them. They need far more attention than do cats. I'd like to pick you up at 3 p.m. if that would be convenient?"

"I'll be standing at the door in my 'farmer-daughter outfit.' Bye for now." Immediately after hanging up, she dialed Brooksie. "Hello, my friend. I have some hopeful news for two of your ladies, Houston and Wilamina. Just got off the phone with Mr. Lagunta and he has a court date for both women. Houston in four months and Wilamina in five months. He will be sending one of his assistants, Ms. Shonte to do some of the interviews. He sounded upbeat about their chances for a new trial and hopefully early release."

"Oh Rachael, wouldn't that be fantastic if they could be found innocent of intentionally killing someone when in fact they were trying to defend a family member. They are both street wise with big hearts. The world would be a better place if there were more Houstons and Wilaminas. In fact, most of the women in my group are fantastic for a variety of reasons. They have had to climb over mountains of garbage since their toddler days. Their strength, courage and perseverance are commendable and amazing. I'm humbled by their bravery."

"A side note to my conversation with Mr. Lagunta. He is taking me to the ranch restaurant you and Luke visited. I must admit, I'm excited and nervous like a school girl going on her first date. Guess we never get too old to worry about the impressions we make."

"I'm also excited for you to experience the restaurant on the most beautiful ranch. There are so many fun things to see and experience. I can't wait to hear your impression. Seems like your attorney friend wants to impress you. He has certainly impressed me with his pro bono work."

"He is full of wonderful surprises. Would you believe he has two cats?"

"Don't let my Aunt Tilly hear that. She'd be dumping a basket full of kittens and mama cat at his doorstep within an hour."

"By the way, how is she and Uncle Joe?"

"They are both fantastic. I think they grow younger every passing year. She has far more energy than I do. I still have dinner with them once a month. Our usual Sunday date is coming up this weekend and I'm taking Luke and Drake for the first time. You know visiting my aunt and uncle is like a visit to the zoo. Drake will be in heaven. I'll love having us all together like a real family."

CHAPTER THIRTY-TWO

**"There is enough in the world
for everyone's need,
but not enough for everyone's greed."**
Frank Buchman, *Remaking the World*.

Janet arrived at work early in order to have time to look at her own stack of bills. She had been worried for months about her personal finances, which was putting more strain and tension on her already unhappy marriage. Riley, her husband of many years, had been gradually increasing his beer intake from one a day to four or six a day. He also had increased his poker playing to three to four times a week. To make matters worse, he was a lousy card player and routinely lost money at each game.

She nervously was straightening Dr. Ronan's desk, picked up a book to move it elsewhere when a piece of paper floated down to the floor. She hurriedly reached for the paper and glanced at the writing. It was her nature to be nosey. The note read, 'meet me at the usual time Thurs. Raintree Park, by the fountain. We've got problems.' There was no signature, but she recognized the handwriting as belonging to Malina Smithers.

Janet had an "aha" moment and thought to herself, *this is a golden opportunity for me to take care of my mounting debts and get the good doctor to finally show some real interest in me, maybe even in us.*

At that very moment, the office door flung open and in walked the doctor. "Janet, what are you doing on the floor?"

"Good morning Dr. Ronan," she palmed the note and quickly stood up. "My usual chore of straightening up your desk. I was simply dusting your desk, and moved a book and out fell this note." Without taking any time to think how to approach the subject of her need of money she opened up her hand and showed the doctor the note.

He grabbed it roughly from her outstretched hand, took a quick peak and responded, "I'm glad you found it or I would have forgotten all about the appointment. Thanks, Janet."

"Doctor, I recognized the handwriting so you don't have to pretend innocent with me. I don't believe your wife or Mrs. Smithers husband would be very happy if they knew about another night meeting between the two of you. I've covered for you many times when Mrs. Ronan would ask me about some of your late night so-called medical appointments. I'm not as stupid as you would like to think."

"I don't know what the hell you are insinuating about, Mrs. Smithers and me."

"Mitchell, I've also covered up and closed my eyes to the missing narcotics and the "alone time" for examinations with some of the inmates, so don't blow any smoke around me. The police asked me if you were ever alone with the younger inmates. I lied for you and now it's your turn to help me out. I'm in a terrible financial bind and you can fix it.

The veins in Dr. Ronan's face and neck were standing out like ropes and his breathing was shallow and loud. He took a menacing step towards his nurse. He stopped abruptly, turned around and locked the office door, then bellowed,

"This is fucking blackmail. You know you have no proof of anything. Your word against mine? Guess who has more clout? Just for the record, how much money are you talking about, for the record you understand?"

Janet was beginning to sweat profusely. She felt the drops between her bra and under her armpits. Her hands were shaking more and more noticeably. "I thought a monthly check of $1500.00 would be fair. That would eventually get me out of the financial hell-hole my husband has put us in."

"I can't believe this is happening. I have always trusted you. How long would you expect a monthly payment?"

"As long as we are working here at Lancers. Your illegal drug transactions must be quite fruitful for you and Mrs. Smithers."

They could both hear the inflow of appointments in the waiting room piling up. Someone yelled out, "Hey, anybody here? You got a roomful of sickos waiting out here."

"We can talk again, Janet, after work today. Right now let's go to work. I'll give you my answer then. I'll be out in a minute after you get the first patient ready."As soon as Janet exited his office, the doctor placed a call to Malina. She answered on the second ring.

"What is it Mitchell?" she asked sounding annoyed.

"Emergency. I must see you at noon. Meet me at my car in the parking lot. Don't be late." he ordered in a high pitched voice.

"Calm down and don't do anything stupid. I'll be there at 12:15."

Parking lot 12:00 p.m..........

Noon time comes and Dr. Ronan can be seen pacing back and forth in front of his Mercedes. Malina arrives a few minutes later, breathing heavily as if she had been running. "Okay Mitchell. I'm here. By the way, you look like a snorting bull eyeing the matador. What the hell is so important?"

They both climbed into his car, shut the doors, he began to explain everything Janet said to him in his office earlier.

"Whoa! What do you mean we? I'm not the drug distributor and I'm not the oversexed idiot fooling around with young inmates."

"Don't think for one second about jumping ship," threatened the doctor. "Our affair and your awareness of drugs being stolen from the infirmary, and not to mention your share of the money, would cost you dearly. You want to be warden, that's a laugh. You are a very willing participant and if I'm caught, I'll make sure you'll get your due credit."

"You're overwrought. Stop and think for a minute. Janet is also an accessory to the activities. She's had a crush on you for a long time. You never give her any hope of becoming one of your conquests. This is all about her jealousy.

"What you do now is to pay attention to her. I'm talking about flirting or more if it becomes necessary, to shut her up. You can afford the monthly payments, but bargain with her. Offer less a month while pinching her butt, and see what happens. Just be sure to pay in cash. Remind her, if she tells anyone the money stops. Also, let her know she will be held partially responsible for the criminal activities because she turned a blind eye."

The doctor squirmed around in the car, wiped his forehead and gripped the steering wheel till his fingers turned white from the pressure. "Malina, I couldn't get it up for her for any reason. I'm not a robot."

"Well my dear doctor, prescribe one of the get up and go pills and do whatever you need to be done to keep her quiet. At least, until we can come up with a better plan. I've got my own hands full with Bo and his fouled up attempt to scare off the facilitators.

We need to watch our every move, for the time being. Don't call me for awhile. I will meet you Sunday night instead of the day we planned, since your hot-for-your-pants nurse found the note and is out in the open now. By the way, I hope you had the sense to burn the note."

The doctor paled even more and stuttered, "Not yet. I was taken by surprise at Janet's nerve and threats. I'll do it when I get back to the office."

"If you have another emergency and feel you must get in touch with me leave a small blank piece of paper under my windshield or call my cell. This will all be okay if we play it safe and smart. Bye until Sunday. Keep your pants zipped, unless of course you are with your evil nurse."

"You really have a sick sense of humor, Malina. Janet is such a bitch. It's not going to be easy to work with her ever again. Don't stand me up on Sunday. I'm not in the mood to be jerked around, not even by you, my love."

CHAPTER THIRTY-THREE

**"If anyone speaks badly of you,
live so no one can believe it."**
Anonymous

Workshop #10

"Welcome ladies," greeted Brooksie. "We have only two more workshops after today. Let's check-in with each of you to see how your personal goals are coming along. After that, we want to review the most meaningful and important topics that will remind you of your self-worth: self-appreciation, self-respect, kindness, accountability, being addiction-free, jobs, parenting, partners, other personal relationships and other topics. The goal of these bi-weekly workshops has been to open your eyes up to see what lovable, gifted, unique children you were, no matter how you were treated or what others said about you. You still have the same potential. You can be lovable, gifted, and unique again, your choice. The ways to demonstrate your specialness is by education, reading, observing, working a job and doing your best at your job, treating everyone, including yourself and other critters with kindness and respect. That means, for example, saying "thank you, please, excuse me, I'm sorry, can I help you", and offering encouragement, sincere compliments and feeling compassion for yourself and others. Compassion is not pity. It is genuinely trying to understand the hurts, disappointments and fears of others, as well as your own."

"We are going to spend a few minutes practicing sincere compliments," announced Lucinda. She turned to Sasha, "Sasha, you have beautiful eyes and shiny hair. Houston, you are a great listener." Now each one of you offer a genuine compliment to one or more of your group.

"Wilamina, you have a beautiful, powerful voice. Sasha, you have a good figure." complimented Corrina.

Each member was able to say several nice remarks about someone in the group. Eventually the women started to make fun of themselves and the others and all the joking around seemed to relax everyone.

Brooksie added, "You may have to practice being kind, respectful and get into the habit of paying sincere compliments. Today when you go through the food line, compliment a worker. Remember, compliments only count if you truly mean them. Now it's time to go over any progress you hopefully have made with the goals you picked. Lucinda is going to read you a list of goals you set for yourselves in workshop 4."

Lucinda spoke to Wilamina, "you wrote down, lose twenty lbs. and read a book. Delores, to learn Spanish and read several biographies about people you find interesting. Corrina, your goal was to lose weight in order to lower your blood pressure. Houston, you wanted to sign up for a business course. Sammy, you spoke of becoming Dr. Blackmore's assistant and you would begin to study books the good doctor was going to send to you. Books to do with what an assistant does. Luella, you stated some interest in agriculture and possibly working in a plant nursery with your dad and studying plants that grow in the Yakima Valley. Charlotte, your goal was to make your mother proud of you and hopefully to visit her. Jackie, your goad was to make your mother as miserable as she had made you. You also added how wonderful and supportive your nanny, Ms. Slauson has been. You wrote that she has been a cheerleader and the person who made you feel loved. Ms. Slauson told you your bitter resentment towards your family was food for cancer. So your nanny's goal for you was to let go of your bitterness and resentment towards family. Berri, you chose losing weight to help reduce your blood pressure and headaches. Sasha, you want to make lots of money and live the easy life plus you might take a business course and someday had a legitimate business."

"Thanks Lucinda for keeping such good notes. We apologize for not asking about progress on your chosen goals before now, but as we said in the first workshop the topics might be switched around as deemed necessary for the what the group was interested in pursuing.

"Now that Lucinda has refreshed your memories, who is willing to share how they did with their intended goals? How difficult was it for you to stay on track? What have you learned about yourself, if anything, concerning setting and attaining personal goals?"

"I'm happy to share that my family is miserable," said Jackie, gleefully with an ear to ear smile. "What does that say about me? Guess I'm one mean, nasty lesbian. Mom has shingles, dad is losing his memory, maybe conveniently, and righteous brother Darion, has been accused of improprieties with a few of the married parishioners. So you can just guess how mortified and humiliated good old mom is. Kent is still the golden boy, living a double life. My dear nanny continues to visit me and writes frequently. She still believes in me. I have been thinking a little bit about what was said about self-forgiveness. But, I'm not sure what I want to forgive myself for?

Brooksie spoke softly, "Jackie, maybe your dear nanny's goal is slowly coming true for you."

"I want to share next 'cause I'm proud," shouted out Wilamina with gusto. "I've lost eighteen pounds. I miss those potatoes something bad, but the scale doesn't."

Congratulations were offered by the group, with noisy enthusiasm.

"I have been studying my Spanish grammar book most every day," shared Delores. "I'm picking it up pretty fast and I picked up a book from the library titled, Evita. She has fascinated me for a long time. Though I can't say I'm learning anything new about myself."

Corrina shared, "I've lost weight. Not as much as Willy, but that's okay. I'll keep on, keeping on, like you said, Brooksie.

"I'm enrolled in a business class. Likin' it so far and I'm catching on to what I'll have to do to run my own agency. Sure are lots of laws and restrictions. Willy and I will get the hang of it and do it all by the book. Mr. Lagunta has given me the name of an accountant who can start us off right. He comes pretty cheap. I bet he's gonna to give us a break because of his friendship with our attorney. Sure some nice guys out there. I just never met any before coming to prison. Ain't that ironic."

"Perhaps things are going better for you, because of the changes you have chosen to make." suggested Brookie.

"Yeah, maybe I'm not expecting shit all the time now. Maybe one day I'll get a box of candy and some roses. Wouldn't that be a kick in the ass." Houston stood up and started to seductively strut around. This got quite a response from the others.

Jackie pointed and laughed heartily, "Hey, careful there girl. You're turning me on." The animated group snorted and laughed and offered a few compliments to Houston's new image.

"Sure feels good to have such lightheartedness for a change. We've been too serious for too long. It's good to be silly and make fools of ourselves," added Brooksie.

Sammy proclaimed, "I study the book that my good vet sent me every night. Sometimes I have to read the same page over and over to get it through my head, what they is saying. I'm slow, but I'm determined to be the best, damn assistant he's ever had or gonna have.

Charlotte said, "I've been writing to my mother. She's pretty sick, but my brother reads her what I write. He tells me she smiles and says she is happy I'm doing better. She hopes to get to hug me soon." Charlotte began to tear up, took a deep breath and added, "I'm trying to get a pass to visit mom and if that don't work, my brother said maybe mom and I can see each other on the computer. He called it scape or skype or something like that."

"I'm glad for you, Charlotte and for me. You're making your mother happy and I wanted my mother to be miserable. Both of us are reaching our goals.

Lucinda asked Luella if she wanted to say anything at this time before the group ended.

"No thank you. I saw my dad on visiting day and he gave me some hard news. I have to chew on it for a while. Maybe next time I can share."

Brooksie affirmed, "Anytime you want to talk, remember Sharon and other group members are good listeners. We'll be back in two weeks, but if you want to talk with Lucinda or me, just call our office. Do you still have our number?"

"Yes ma'am I do and thanks."

The inmates gradually left the table, but continued to joke around with each other. Sharon and the team of facilitators, hugged, said their good-byes. When the facilitators got out to the parking area, Tony was waiting to escort them safely back to the Grief Clinic.

CHAPTER THIRTY-FOUR

"It is not love that is blind, but jealousy."
Lawrence Durrell, *Justine*

When the Warden arrived at work, she was greeted by Detectives Yomoto and Rowe in the prison parking area. There were two patrol cars with lights flashing. The officers had situated themselves in front and in back of Janet Black's car.

"What's going on here?" worriedly asked the Warden, looking at the detectives.

"We received a anonymous call to check out Mrs. Black's car as soon as she had parked and gone through the gates to the infirmary. The caller stated that we would find a container of narcotics and cash. We hurriedly obtained a warrant, then drove here with police backup. I had just placed a call to the infirmary asking Mrs. Black to come down to the parking area and bring her purse and car keys with her. You have arrived before she's had time to get here. Here she comes through the gate."

Janet moved quickly in front of the detectives brandishing her purse. "What's this all about? Why do you want me here? You've nearly scared me to death. Did my husband set you on me? I threw him out of the house last night, because he was stinking drunk again, I've had it with him. This is the last straw."

"Slow down, Mrs. Black. We are here to inspect your car." He showed her the warrant and asked her for the car key.

"Why in the world do you want to look in my car? Something is very wrong here. Warden, do I have to let them?" Janet looks pleadingly over at the Warden.

"Janet, they have a warrant and yes, you must cooperate. Please hand Detective Yomoto your keys."

Janet fumbled and dropped her purse. One of the officers bent down to retrieve the purse and bumped heads with Janet. "Sorry ma'am." He handed the purse back to Janet, who then handed it to the detective. Her hands were trembling. She was asked to take the keys out of her purse which she did. Placed them in Yomoto's out-stretched hand. He handed them off to the nearest police officer and instructed him to begin the search.

As soon as the trunk was opened, the detectives were called over to look at what had been discovered.

The Warden had been standing with Janet trying to reassure her the search would be over soon and she could get back to work. Detective Yomoto walked back from behind the car and announced to Janet, in his cop-like voice, "I'm going to read you your rights," which he did and then continued, "I'm placing you under arrest and I'm having your car impounded as evidence for possession of narcotics and an undisclosed large amount of cash."

All color left Janet's face and she stumbled, nearly falling down. The Warden grabbed her to keep her upright. "What the hell are you talking about? I've no idea where that stuff came from. There has been some terrible mistake. There's no way my dead beat husband could have any cash. I know he couldn't have done this." Janet became quiet, looked up to one window in particular on the second floor of the prison. I want a lawyer waiting for me at your station. I'm not saying another word to anyone without my lawyer. Just you wait, Detective, 'cause I'm going to sing like a bird, loud and clear. You have a surprise coming."

Janet was heard mumbling to herself as she was being led to the police car, "They're not going to get away with this shit. I'll talk like a magpie. Just you wait."

Warden James looked dazed. She stared into space, most of the color had drained from her face. Detective Rowe asked her to please sit down in the patrol car, "Warden, you look quite pale and unsteady."

"I can't believe Janet is selling hospital drugs. She sounded like she was talking crazy about them not getting away with it. Who is 'them'? What a mess."

In a gentle voice, Detective Yomoto, directed the warden to follow Detective Rowe. "Detective Rowe will stay with you, 'til you feel more in charge. You may have some questions and Detective Rowe can fill you in and catch you up to date. As soon as I have more information you will get a call from one of us. Looks like the good doctor's nurse is going to become as she puts it, a song bird, a magpie."

Within fifteen minutes the Warden thanked and dismissed Detective Rowe. She made a call to Dr. Ronan. She told the him she would get a substitute for Janet as soon as possible, but in the meantime the infirmary will remain closed except for emergencies.

He asked what happened to Janet. She told him that she was arrested for possessing drugs and cash that were found in her car. "You can't be serious. She has been my right hand for a long time. She's no criminal. This is some crazy mistake, crazy mistake."

"Mitchell, just do as I asked. Close the infirmary until another nurse shows up. Shouldn't be more than an hour or so."

The Warden dialed Mela Washington, the night nurse, and briefly explained the situation and asked her if she could she double back and work another shift. Mela agreed readily, thinking to herself it would be an opportunity to check out Dr. Ronan.

At the police station.....

At the police station, Janet had already obtained a lawyer, a public defender by the name of Miss Gordon. The attorney was unsuccessfully trying, to quiet down her new client and have her simply answer the questions. It seemed Janet had already figured out who had planted the drugs and cash in her car and she couldn't wait to expose them. *They think they are smarter than me. Boy, oh boy! will they be surprised at just how much I know about them. He'll be sorry he tried to use me, to fool me and to make a fool out of me.*

"I'm ready to answer your questions now, Miss Gordon, I'm also ready to give you all the evidence you'll need to catch the real criminals. I hope you have enough paper to write down all I have to say. Their butts are going to feel the heat and I'm about to light the fire. Little old me."

CHAPTER THIRTY-FIVE

**"You've got to learn to leave the table
when love's no longer being served."**
Nina Simone

Workshop 11

Brooksie began the session, " You are captain of your own ship, no matter the weather, the obstacles, or any other unforeseen circumstances. You are in charge. You make the decisions. You are responsible, but only for the actions you take, not for other people's choices, actions or behaviors.

"Today we want you to focus on three points: support options, job prospects and self-image. We have discussed all of these before, so today is a brush up. We will be reviewing the people and systems you plan to lean on when you need some encouragement or direction. What good quality or qualities have you recently discovered about yourself. If any? Most of you picked one or more of the inmates in this group for your options. A few of you chose a family member, friend, a lawyer, an old employer or Lucinda and me. By the way, Lucy and I are both pleased and honored that you would consider us as part of your support system. We will make sure you have our contact information on or before our last session. When you made these choices in workshop #6, have you added any new ones or gotten rid of the ones you shared with us?

If you've forgotten what support you spoke of before, Lucinda can refresh your memory. She's the best note keeper.

"I would like to add Sammy's veterinarian, Dr. Blackmore, as one of my support people. He seems to be one of the good guys." said Houston. "Maybe I'll have some pets someday. I would take them to him and I could talk easy with Sammy. She's okay in my book."

Brooksie addressed Houston, "Would you be okay sharing how long you believe you will continue your incarceration here at Lancers, now that you are working with Mr. Longunta?"

"Mr. Lagunta tells me I may possibly be looking for a job in the next six months or so."

Wilamina interrupted her friend, "He said almost the same to me, Tex. He actually said six months to a year." She choked up and added, "I thought I was going to leave this place buried in the poor man's graveyard, feet first. Praise the Lord! I got a chance for living, loving, singing and now even helping others. Thank you Jesus." Her broad shoulders shook. She swiped her sleeve over her wet cheeks and under her nose. "Hallelujah! I'm going to be a business woman. Me and Houston we're gonna scare the shit out of those no goods. I'm already feeling sorry for all those bullies when me and Houston find them and drag their sorry asses off to jail."

"You're so right, partner. We're gonna clean the streets. I still think my best support comes from Mr. Lagunta, Sharon, Willy, you and Lucinda plus my brothers. I'll soon finish the business accounting course here. My oldest brother told me I can stay at his place till I get on my feet. He also has a friend in the window washing business and that guy will give me a job. I figure I can work for him a year, hang my hat at my brother's and save every penny. By then, Willy should be out and we could rent a small office and start up our new business. In that time I can work on getting a P.I. license and whatever else we need to put on our sign, "The Salt and Pepper Investigative Agency." Willy you can stay with me at my brother's house. We each can have our own bedroom and share a bathroom. We'll become his housekeepers and cooks in payment for room and board.

"My self-image is about the same. I'm still loyal and hardworking. What has changed for me since this program..........." she hesitates, folds her hands in handshake fashion and looks at Sharon, "I have hope for a future. I am a decent person and I'm going to make one hell of a honest and fair investigator. Doing my best for the underdog and my worst for the bully."

"Hey Tex, your agency is the first place I'll head for if I ever find myself in trouble," blasted Sammy. "If my employer has any problems, the first thing I'll do is send him to you and Willy."

Sammy continued, "The people I trust are still Dr. Blackmore, Houston, Wilamina and Sharon, who shouldn't even be here in the first place. She only acted in kindness for her sick-in-the-head sister. I trust Brooksie, Lucinda and my friend on the outside. She was always worried about my partner's mental condition. She told me many times, 'a broken arm is fixable, but a broken mind, that's something else'.

"I know what job I got waiting for me. I've been reading the books the good doctor sent to me. I'm getting smarter every day. I'd rather die than let the doc down. I'm like Houston, loyal and hard working. I'll give all I have to help the animals.

"Not sure about my good qualities, I never thought I'd become someone with a decent job title, let alone, somebody's assistant. I'm not a quitter, that's good, ain't it?"

Lucinda jumped up and moved to Sammy, hugged her tightly and said, "You are definitely not a quitter and that's a great quality."

Sammy looked down at her feet to retie a shoe lace that didn't need to be retied. "Thanks Lucy. Sorry I mean Lucinda. I didn't mean to be using your nickname."

"I'm flattered to hear you call me Lucy, like maybe we're becoming friends."

"Hell, if you wasn't straight we could be real good friends," chided Sammy.

Lucinda turned a rapidly changing color from pinkish to tomato red. It began to color her nose first and then moved all around her neck and ended up on the tips of her ears. Everyone began to laugh and Lucinda said, "I take that as a compliment Sammy, you'd be a great catch."

"Jackie, do you still consider Mrs. Slauson, Sharon, and Mela Washington your support options?" asked Brooksie.

"Oh yes absolutely. Mrs. Slauson has always treated me with love. She is loyal, kind and loves me like a real parent, like a good mother would. Sharon and Mela are both wise and smart and give me sensible suggestions. I'm beginning to see myself more like how Mrs. Slauson sees me, not like the way my parents do. Too much religion has made them mean. My older brother is arrogant and my younger brother is a liar, a hypocrite. My friends in here are at least honest. So, I guess I can say I'm becoming a more honest person and I like myself for that."

In her abrupt style, Charlotte stated, "My brother first and then the Warden. She has been straight with me since I first got here. Then I guess a few of you guys, maybe. I've always been a hard working woman, just like my mom. This program has given me a kick in the butt to keep working hard and take advantage of the classes offered. I'm gonna be okay and do right for myself, my mom and brother. I just got stupid for a time. When I get out of here and if I ever have another boyfriend, he's going have to be a working machine. He's at least got to be willing to do as much as I do."

"You sound so much more enthusiastic about your future today which warms my heart. You made a mistake and I believe you have learned from it. That's more than many others on the outside have done. I applaud your fighting spirit," complimented Brooksie.

"Corinna, would you care to share your thoughts?" asked Lucinda.

"You bet. I trust this prison group. And that includes both of you ladies. But you can believe I don't want anything to do with those church going folks. They have caused me more pain and thrown more blame at me than any of the so-called criminals living in here behind bars. The real crooks are out there preaching. Maybe it's not my fault, my baby died. I'm trying to forgive myself and forgive God for not saving her."

"Oh honey, don't you worry anymore about being forgiven. That happened long ago and God never stopped loving you. I know you hate it when I start saying Amen, but you're just one more child of God, like the rest of us. Some of us hurt others, some hurt themselves, but we're all just God's children and doing our best, " humbly offered Wilamina.

"Thanks Willy, I know you mean well," added Corrina.

Delores commented, "I still consider my folks and their minister my best shot at support. I've learned a few things about myself like how to stay out of trouble when I eventually get out of here. I'm not trying to get my R.N. license reinstated, I've decided to go another route when I'm turned loose. I'm going to work with addicts, since I've first-hand knowledge and know all the excuses and ins and outs of the drug world."

"Would you continue to attend AA or NA meetings when you're back home?" asked Brooksie.

"Sure, if the gate keepers said I needed to. I'll do what it takes to stay clean outside," answered Delores.

"Sasha, what about you?" asked Brooksie.

"You're not going like my answer 'cause it is the same as before. Not saying I haven't heard what all of you have been telling me, but I have my own history and my own path. I'll stick with my uncle and maybe find me a new pimp, one less horny, but more honest."

Berri laughed heartily and contended, "I've never met an honest pimp. Good luck to you Sasha, you're going to need it. I'd probably go to Tex and Willy when they get their office open. I have a good feeling about the Warden and the nurse, Mela. She works at night. She's always been straight with me."

"Luella, you and Wilamina are the last two to share, " said Lucinda.

"I'm closest to my dad. He has been my friend forever. But at the last visiting day, he asked me to do something real hard. This is as good a time as any to tell you what my dad wants me to do, here goes. He wants me to sign papers giving up my two daughters to a foster family who want to adopt them. I've been thinking hard about it. A social worker came to visit me and told me all about the foster family who have been caring for my kids for the past two years. I'm afraid my girls will hate me when they grow up, knowing I gave them away, like an old dress. My dad and I cried. He said they have a much better chance for a good life with the foster family than with me, 'cause I don't know how long I'll be here. I could be here for five more years, maybe longer. I know I was a bad addict, and not much of a mother. It's tearing my guts out to decide." As she was talking, her face was glistening with sweat and tears. She sat silently and stared down at the floor.

No one spoke for a long time. Finally Berri spoke up, almost in a whisper,

I have called you some bad names in the past and I'm sorry about that, but this must be a really hard decision. What did the social worker say about the people who want to adopt your kids?"

"She said they are teaching my kids English and Spanish. They take them to a Catholic Church on Sunday. They are not able to have their own children, some female problem with the lady and that they have wanted children for a long time. They let my dad see his grandchildren once a month and he says they are kind and loving. He says my kids seem so happy with them.

"I don't want them to become a junkie like me. My mother couldn't help me do right 'cause she had a brain problem. My dad worked twelve to sixteen hours a day to support us. I was lonely and took to the gang life."

"What is your heart telling you to do?" asked Wilamina?

Luella began to sob in earnest. Most of the group remained quiet. While others shed tears. They waited patiently for Lu to start talking again.

"My heart tells me to give them a chance for a future with two loving people. My dad can see them two or three times a year until they turn eighteen. Then it will be up to Anna and Rachael if they want to keep seeing him. If I'm out then, they can also see me if they want to."

"This may be the hardest decision you'll ever have to make. It will take courage and one big heart filled with love for your children. One day they may understand just how much love it took for you to give them away. Your two greatest treasures! You're going to have much grief and we will see that you receive all the support you need for that. Some women in this group may become listeners and sounding boards for you. After all, you have a 'captured audience' in here and I've seen some wonderful friendships blossom and grow! Whatever you decide, you can receive support. The Warden, your dad, Dr. Gibran, along with the friends you've made in here. All will be good sources for you to draw upon."

Wilamina was the last one to talk about her ideas of support and she chose to show support for Luella by singing 'You Raise Me Up' by Brendan Graham and Rolf Lovland. A beautiful piece with powerful, uplifting words expressing spiritual support.

The group dispersed after many tissues were soaked, followed by hugs and good wishes.

Sasha..........

Sasha waited till the others were out of ear shot, then she moved next to Brooksie. In a barely discernible whisper said, "Someone handed this to me and asked me to give it to you." She pushed it hard into Brooksie's hand and with amazing speed took a place in the waiting food line.

Brooksie hesitated briefly than slipped the note into the pocket of her sweater. As soon as she and Lucy were out of the cafeteria, she told her friend about the note. They swiftly went through the restroom door and checked to see if they were alone. No one else was in there at the moment, so they took the time to read the note. It said 'Heads up'.

"My God! we need to get this to the Warden now. Lucinda asked one of the CO's to take them to the Warden's office, which she did.

Brooksie knocked on the Warden Jame's door, "Come in," responded the Warden. As soon as the door closed behind them, Brooksie handed the note over to the Warden. "Sasha handed me this and said someone asked her to hand it to one of us." Immediately after the Warden read the warning words, she thanks and dismissed the facilitators. "I'll get back to you later. Thanks and have a safe trip home." She quickly dialed the detectives.

Detective Rowe answered the phone. "Detective, I have received a note reading 'Heads up'. I will have the inmate sent to my office under some sort of pretense. "We'll be in your office within the next half hour and thanks, Warden."

In the meantime, Sasha was being accompanied to the Warden's office by one of the new undercover CO's. The CO remained outside the office door as Sasha entered and took a seat.

"Sasha, we have to wait for the detectives. They should be arriving at any moment. When you return to the cafeteria you can say you received a emergency call about your uncle."

"Oh no, did my dear uncle finally have that heart attack that we've been expecting for a long time now? He is fat, drinks too much and smokes like a chimney. He's a heart attack just waiting to happen."

Detective Yomoto and his partner came through the door before the Warden had a chance to answer Sasha. The detectives seated themselves, after shaking hands with Sasha. "Now you know the identity of our very talented plant."

"You mean Sasha is actually a policewoman? I can't believe it. You have one hell of a reputation as a happy ho, Sasha," remarked the Warden.

"Yes ma'am I do my best to be convincing. My cell mate Maxine Ritter told me, just before I left for the group program that there was a plan to cut the brake line on the your car tomorrow, soon after you arrived at work. I didn't think it wise to ask many questions so I had to act disinterested. That pissed off Maxine because she has a need to be in the lime light. After a few moments Maxine added, "You'll never believe where I heard that."

So I said "I bite, where?" She said, "I was in the docs office and in comes Lorelie, so named the black widow. You know the one who is being sent to England for murdering her husband?

Anyway, we chatted back and forth, awaiting our turn to see Dr. "horny". She told me he will do anything for her to get into her pants. He told her last time she visited him about some rumors going around to get rid of the Warden. Maxine then said that he said anything can be done with hard cash or drugs. Then he told her about the brakes getting cut on a certain date. Turns out that tomorrow is the date. Maxine also said that, 'I don't mind the old gal getting hers. She's never done nothing for me."

"So you believe this Black Widow person?"

"You bet I do. She's got all the moves that seem to make the guys go stupid. I've run into her several times in Dr. Ronan's office. I've seen her wrap him around her finger. She thinks she's something special and guess he does too. His nurse doesn't like her much, probably jealous."

"Guess time will tell if what Maxine told me is fact or rumor. See you later. I'm off to my Wednesday group. By the way Warden, In my humble opinion, I think the workshops are great and are doing something to help our inmates see themselves. It also sparks hope in them for a better future. I'm learning a few valuable lessons for me personally as well.. Hope you can keep the workshops available for a long time. I think they will make a difference, at least for some."

CHAPTER THIRTY-SIX

**"You are richer today if you have
laughed, given or forgiven."**
Anonymous

Facilitators meet for lunch.....

Brooksie informed her friends of a telephone message she received, "Sharon called me a few days back to remind us to bring fifty copies of the program assessment form. She would like to hand them out herself at the end of our last workshop. She wants to have a meeting later in the week with the twenty inmates and have them complete the forms then. She also has plans to have different staff members complete the form. Employees from the cafeteria, the infirmary and the COs. After a few weeks she will give us the results of the assessments from the inmates perspectives and the staff's including the Warden's.

"Personally, I have seen some remarkable progress from most of the ten woman. I don't believe they've have been putting on an act, but I guess that is possible. Most have probably felt they had to do con jobs in order to get by. I hope and pray they didn't feel it necessary to play games with us. Even Sasha had some sincere moments. I'm curious why Sasha was the one who gave us the note. Who gave it to her? It had to be someone she didn't want to refuse. She's acting pretty tough, but the plant must be tougher.

I wouldn't want to go undercover in this prison. These women can be a force to deal with if they don't like you or worse yet, if they feel betrayed. If she is actually a policewoman, she's one hell of an actor."

"No." answered Lucinda. "I would never believe that she was the undercover person. She told such a believable and horrific childhood story. You just can't make that kind of stuff up. Hope we eventually are told who the plant is."

"I feel positive myself about the inmates in our group as well. At times, Anita and I were awed by the insights they shared with us," added Rachael. "Their stories sadly opened my eyes to another world. Made me think again about the need for all to get licensed after a few years of training, before having children. It boils down to what kind of parents you have and how each individual responds to the variety of child-raising techniques. It's really a luck of the draw."

Anita suggested, "I would like to see us have some kind of graduation party after the last workshop. What do you all think? I can run off a nice graduation certificate and give them each some type of special gift. Maybe like new combs, hairbrushes or a gift certificate to the prison's beauty salon. They could have a shampoo, hair cut, even permanent if they wanted to."

"We definitely need to do something special for the inmates, the Warden and Sharon," offered Lucinda. "What if we brought pizza and Tony could make his fantastic cakes or pies for dessert?"

"We should get the Warden to agree to whatever we decide to do. Maybe she would have some ideas to offer us. Dr. Gibran and her nurse, Mela could be included in the party as well." added Brooksie. "Who would like to call the Warden with our requests?"

"Don't all answer at once you guys. Okay I get it. I'll call her today and let you know what she says."

The friends continued brain storming for the last upcoming workshop and how much they've enjoyed working with Sharon and her worthwhile project.

Brooksie thoughtfully said, "I'm going to miss Sharon and the amazing women in our group. I believe I've learned far more from them than they have learned from me. I admit, I'm so excited about the investigative agency Houston and Wilamina are planning to open as soon as they can. I pray nothing goes wrong at their retrials. Sammy is another person I hope will keep in contact with us. She's so determined to do a great job for her vet and the animals. The Warden is working on the possibility of the inmates working with dogs from the shelters. My Aunt Tilly is lining up a few shelters who want to participate. They would supply the dogs and possibly recommend trainers. Actually, I feel like a mother hen for all ten women in my group. I want to be able to see them years from now living healthy fulfilled lives, surrounded by loving family and friends, feeling great about themselves and what they are contributing to society."

The others agreed in unison. They reminded each other to be observant at all times, not to take any chances, and lastly, to have a great weekend until they meet again for the last workshop. All agreed that having Tony and Luke as their drivers/bodyguards has made them feel so much safer. It's been a wonderful opportunity to get to know the guys better.

"Before we go our separate ways, I need to let you know Luke and I have set the date for the month of September. The wedding ceremony is going to be at my house, outside on the patio and the feast or reception will be at Luke's place. His family, my aunt and uncle, Sharon and the Warden will attend by Skype. You three with your dates. Luke's son will be the ring bearer. Lucinda do you think Tony's daughter would like to be the flower girl? My uncle will walk me down the garden path. Anita, your brother is also invited if he wants to come."

"She will be so excited and Tony will be honored, like me," answered Lucinda.

"This is not going to be a fancy affair so you don't need to go out and buy anything new. I'm going to wear a white suit. The skirt will be knee length, with a white silk blouse and assorted flowers in my hair. My dear dogs and cats will be part of the audience, although they won't be invited to the reception. I'm keeping that secret from them. Oh, I forgot! My two favorite neighbors are also invited. They have been good friends and terrific neighbors since I moved in next door to them. You met them at our last Christmas party here."

"Do I remember" You bet I do! Who could possibly forget what great dancers and attentive hosts they were," chimed in Rachael.

The next half hour sounded like the four friends had turned back the clock, and were all in their twenties again. Several talking at the same time, asking questions, offering congratulations and finally got down to the nitty gritty question, 'what should I wear'? Happy talk and all sort of plans finally concluded with good-byes and hugs ended at their own cars.

CHAPTER THIRTY-SEVEN

"Be yourself; everyone else is already taken."
Oscar Wilde (1854-1900)

Visiting day with the attorney..........

Houston, Wilamina and Susie Wu were all displaying their own individual outward signs of nervousness. Susie was practically chewing her nails down to the quick, Wilamina was humming, not so softly, a gospel hymn and Houston was crossing and uncrossing her legs and arms, often simultaneously. She nearly caused herself to fall off the bench. This near accident triggered giggles from the other two.

"What's so funny you two?" asked Houston.

"You are Tex. You're moving around like frog legs in a hot frying pan," responded Willy.

"Hell, I'm so nervous and I admit scared shitless. I'm counting on leaving this place soon. Don't know what I'll do if I get bad news." She patted Susie on the back and said, "One thing for sure, you'd better get good news quick or your fingers are in danger of disappearing."

Susie looked at her fingertips, "I can't break the habit when I'm anxious. Maybe I should start wearing gloves anytime I think I might get bad news."

At that very moment the clerk asked Susie to go into room #3.

"Best of luck, Susie," offered the other two at the same time.

A short time later, Susie returned to the hall with a Cheshire cat grin stretching from ear to ear on her petite face. She made a thumbs up and wished them both good luck.

Houston was called in next. Before she stood up she grabbed Willy's hands, squeezed them tightly, and remained silent. Moisture was forming in Willy's eyes and she said, "Amen, my sister."

Mr. Lagunta was standing when she entered the small room. "I'm not going to prolong your anxiety. Our case is strong. We go in front of a judge in six weeks and I believe you will be a free woman soon after that. Best case scenerio is that he judge will overturn your previous charges and a new trial date will be given. Then, you should then be set free on bail and a new date for the trial will be set. My staff is already working on contacting witnesses and other pertinent information for your new trial."

"How can I ever repay you? You're giving me my life back," exclaimed Houston.

"I believe once your agency is up and running I will send you some clients. I know you will work your ass off for them and that will be more than enough payment. See you next Monday so we can go over what you can expect to hear from the judge. I will also have a few more questions of my own at that time."

"Can I ask if Willy is going to get good news like me?"

"Yes she is. Please ask the clerk to send her in as you are leaving."

Houston couldn't hardly remember walking out of the interview room. "I'm going to be free from these walls in six weeks. Can't believe it." She was shaking her head back and forth when she saw her friend looking up at her. Willy started to wring her hands and then she let out a wail.

Houston immediately shouted out, "We're going to be in business together some time this year. Go on in and see our 'guardian angel' and hear the news for yourself."

"Hallalujah! my heart gonna pop right out of this ugly grey shirt." Wilamina practically floated all the way to the doorway where the lawyer was waiting, with a smile.

"Hello Wilamina." He said while backing away, anticipating what may be coming from this demonstrative woman. "By the look on your face, I assume your friend shared the good news."

"Sir. I just gotta hug you before I burst." Mr. Lagunta opened his arms and hoped he'd have enough breath left after her bear-like hug.

"Now to your news. We will be in the courtroom eight weeks from today, two weeks after Houston. You will be in front of the judge who is to decide if you will be granted a retrial. As I told Houston, I believe he will grant us a new trial date at that time. He will set bail for you and then you will be permitted to leave prison until your new trial begins. I will need to see you every Monday for a while with more questions and to prepare you for what's coming from the judge. Do you have anyone who can furnish you with a new outfit? I forgot to mention this to Houston, could you please relay this to her?

"Yes sir, I'll figure out something right away and I'll give Houston your message. I'm so grateful. How am I gonna make this up to you? I can clean your house, work in the yard or whatever you need doing."

"Houston already asked me the same question and I'm going to give you the same answer. Work hard in your new business. I'll send you clients. That will be payment enough."

She bear hugged him one more time and gave multiple blessings, while backing out of the room. Wilamina wasn't ten feet away from the door when she broke into her favorite hymn, 'Amazing Grace'. She could be heard all the way to the cafeteria.

CHAPTER THIRTY-EIGHT

"You must be true to yourself. Strong enough to be true to yourself. Brave enough to be strong enough to be true to yourself. Wise enough to be brave enough, to be strong enough to shape yourself from what you actually are."
Sylvia Constance Ashton-Warner, New Zealander Author and Educator (1908-84)

Workshop 12..........

Graduation Day.

The inmates were assembling in the cafeteria for their last workshop. Compared to previous workshops, they were noticeably subdued.

"Welcome ladies and friends to our final workshop. You might notice a few extra tissue boxes scattered around. These are mainly for Lucinda and me. We are both wimps when it comes time for good-byes. The hours spent with you all have been both an honor and a privilege for Lucy and me. You have bravely and generously shared bits of your lives with us and have taught us a great deal about the cruelties that were done to you during childhood and the lasting effects they've had on you. Most amazing is the courage you've all shown by not simply hanging it all up.

"I have been inspired by your bravery to survive and fight on a daily basis from past horrific experiences. I'm reminded of a story I heard long ago. There was a new baby horse born. The mama horse and the people who owned the horses were supposed to care for the newborn. Instead, the baby was neglected, made fun of, frightened, yelled at and pushed away. The mama horse didn't want to let the baby suckle. The humans said the baby was defective. Some made fun of the youngster, pointing out that she had short legs, a broomstick looking tail and mane, and elephant like ears. Even the other young horses wouldn't play with the new one. One year later the young horse continued to be friendless, but had learned the joy of running. Her short legs, were strong and fast. One day, a gate was left open and she ran into the nearby forest. She ran and ran and never looked back. She learned to eat off the land and remained alone. Time passed and she made a few bad choices. She found herself in a desert with little water to drink. Another time, she found herself high upon a high mountain covered in snow with no grass to eat. She kept on running until one day she found a green valley with water running through it.

Then a human appeared. She saw him and remembered how badly she had been treated so she took off running like the wind. The human was so impressed with her agility and speed that he decided to try to befriend her. It took some coaxing. Eventually, with patience and kindness plus a few apples and sugar cubes, he earned her trust and he took her to his ranch. He was a kind and gentle sort of person who had been rescuing abused horses for many years. He named the new horse, Mariah, after the song about the wind. She had a few scars, both inside her heart and outside her body, but my God, how she could run! Some time passed and Mariah was entered into a race. She gave it her all, beat the other horses by a mile and then to her surprise, the kind man called her a champion and placed a beautiful wreath around her neck. This short legged, mangy tail and mane, outcast, unloved and mocked horse was a champion. Standing in the Winner circle, with her head held high, and multiple scars from bites and kicks still visible. It no longer mattered to her. She had earned medals of honor and bravery. She was a true winner after all.'

"I'm not comparing any of you to a horse, but I see you all as winners. You've not given up and now you're learning to be the hero of your own story. Day by day, you have been willing to look at your own potential and work to uncover it."

Some sniffing and nose blowing could be heard around the table. Sharon wiped her nose and dabbed at her cheeks with a much used tissue and said, "That story represents exactly what I had in mind for this program. I believe no matter how old someone is if they will simply believe in their own self-worth and potential, they can and will enter the Winner's circle. It takes a great deal of courage and perseverance plus the understanding that you cannot fail if you refuse to give up.

"You will be handed a survey and I ask you to please fill it out and write any other comments you may have. Positive or negative remarks or suggestions will be greatly appreciated and considered for the next program. Six months and one year from now you will receive another similar questionnaire to fill out. The goals of these workshops have been to teach you how to respect yourself regardless of your life experiences, to see your potential, how to begin to develop your strengths, how to be your own best friend and how to forgive yourself for the multiple and harmful choices."

Brooksie asked, " Do any of you feel differently about yourself today than you did six months ago? Anyone?"

Houston responded, "I'm no longer a murderer. I'm a defender. I'm sorry I killed a human being, but I'm glad I saved someone's life. For the very first time I can see myself in a job with purpose."

Her voice began to crack and she took another deep breath. "I have my first no bullshit friends, Willy and a few others whom I believe have my back. You know who you are and I would go to the mat for you as well. Guess I never admitted how lonely my life was, but no more!"

Silence hung heavy in the corner of the mess hall till Willy shouted out, "hallalujah! I've got a friend now besides Jesus. This one I can see and soon we will be the amazing investigators."

Berri spoke up after wiping her face with her sleeve. "I do have something to offer now. I'm not a waste. If I remain here forever I can still make a difference. Taking a few classes and getting into the dog rescue training class. It's supposed to begin in the next five months. Maybe the dogs I get to work with can make others happy and safe. That would make me feel like I was making a good contribution. My life would mean something and my Ali would know how much I love him and how much I miss him. He could be proud of his mama."

"Absolutely Berri, and maybe my baby in heaven can ask God to send me another baby to love and care for," said Corinna. "I'm not such a bad person, just because some people said I was doomed to hell, I don't think I really care what they think anymore. I know I've made lots of mistakes and I'm going try to not do'em again. I can put my good memory to work and take several classes.

I'd like to work with babies, in a doctor's office or something like that. I'm losing weight and that makes me feel good."

Sammy raised her hand and said, "I am different today than I was six months ago. I have something to give, not only to pets. I want to live for a long time. Before I didn't care if I never woke up again. In fact, many mornings I didn't want to wake up. I have a f...... future now, and I'm going to make the doc proud, maybe even famous".

"I can say, " announced Charlotte, "I don't think so little of myself today. I've always thought that just because I could work hard for long hours, made me look like a dumb ox. The ox can pull tons and for a long time, but he's looked upon like a stupid animal who don't know better. That's how everyone saw me, like a work horse or an ox. No brains, no feelings, just meant for hard work. Mom got my letter and my brother said she cried and told him to tell me she's proud of me because I keep trying to do better. She told him she's not afraid to die now, 'cause she knows I'm gonna be okay." Charlotte forcibly blew into the tissue and wiped her eyes. She graced the group with her best smile and a wink.

"You're somethin', girl. Your mama taught you good. I'm happy for you and her," shouted out Willy. "I know I'm better now 'cause I have a friend who believes in me and wants me to be her business partner. I gotta add that I feel close to everyone in this group and that's includes Miss Sharon, and you two teachers. I know you said you ain't teachers, but you sure as hell have taught some good stuff. Sounds like teaching to me. I pray to Jesus for forgiveness for what I did to Armon and I pray for him too. He was hell-bent on killing my baby brother. My brother is trying to do right and he has thanked me for saving him. That makes me feel good. All I see coming down the road in front of me is good living and a world full of hurt for dirt bags that Tex and I corral. Shit, I'm already beginning to sound like a Texan."

"I'm going to miss you Willy," expressed Sasha. "Most of you have changed a lot. Can't say I have, but I can say I see more opportunities for me. The street life looks different to me now. Who knows what the future is going to hold. The road I decide to follow may surprise me."

Delores said to Sasha, "If I looked as good as you do, maybe I'd become a ho, but I don't look sexy, so I won't go down that road. I've learned that my parents lived for Rick, the baby of the family, and Dan and I were both second class citizens. In their eyes, we could never measure up to Rick. That used to hurt me, but no more. Rick was special in every way. He was smart, handsome, athletic, funny, popular and religious. He was perfect and they've never gotten over his death. I doubt they'll even cry at my funeral. Maybe they will shed a tear or two for Dan, and then quickly forget him and talk about their other son, Rick. I'll find my own road and I'll do okay. I'm thinking of becoming an accountant. I'm real good with numbers."

Jackie looked directly at Delores and said, "We're still both hung up on our Bible thumping parents. Least that's how it sounds to me, Delores. At least now you say they can't hurt you anymore. I hope you mean that. I feel differently now. Six months ago I was pissed every day. I went to bed mad and woke up mad. Not sure why that was, but my stomach doesn't hurt as much anymore. Kent can live his double life and take money living a lie. That is his life, not mine and I believe I can let it go. My minister brother is a stranger to me and as far as I'm concerned, he can stay a stranger. When I get out of here, I plan on living my own life and basically stay as far away from all four of them as possible. Maybe I will find someone I can love and she will love me back. Then I will have a family. A family of two people who care about the other's happiness. I've made some friends here. I hope we can stay in contact. I wish the best for Houston and Willy, when they get their business started. You're both good women and I'm glad I've gotten to know you and the rest of you in this group."

"Luella would you like to say something?" asked Lucinda.

"Yes ma'am. But, I'm afraid I'll start crying and won't stop. Never thought I would say this," she grabbed a handful of tissues and stared at the picture she was holding. "I'm going to give up my kids. I signed the papers yesterday. The social worker tried to comfort me and said the adoption will take about six months. She thanked me for doing the best for my girls. Now they will have a new mother, a good mother." She stared at nothing for a long moment, then glanced at the picture she was holding. "Do you guys want to see my kids?"

Unanimously the group said, "Yes." The picture was passed around slowly and very thoughtfully from one hand to the next. The two inmates who had experienced the loss of children were softly crying. Brooksie stood up, walked a short distance turning her back to the group. Her shoulders quaking.

"You're a good mother, a good person, Luella. You've done right by your precious girls. It took guts and love for you to sign those papers," Berri said kindly. "I bet your dad is real proud of you."

Luella's voice broke when she said, "Yeah he is and he's broken up just like me." Her chin started trembling again and she dug around for tissues. Berri quickly handed her a few and touched her gently on one shoulder.

Brookie had finally returned to her seat, red-eyed and sniffling. "This pilot program has been a great success, in my opinion. I know Lucy and the other two facilitators agree wholeheartedly with me. We are proud of all of you and Sharon. Also proud to be a part of such a worthwhile project. I told you before, that we hope to stay in touch with you by mail or phone. You can call us at the number or write us at the address shown on the cards Lucy passed out earlier. I believe I can speak for the other three when I say we will answer any of your letters or calls. It would be a privilege to be pen pals with you.

"Now we will be joined by the other group and end this last workshop with some special treats, we have pizza and four great desserts made by Lucy's baking husband. Certificates will be handed out to each one of you with a special note written on the back. Our combined wish for each of you is to daily remember how unique and valued you are and to never rest working toward your special potential."

Cheers, chattering and laughter continued for the next hour. It was party time and graduate inmates, staff and facilitators alike were joyful and hungrily devoured the treats.

The Warden signaled for the facilitators to follow her back to her office as the celebrations continued.

The Warden began, "This has been a very successful project and I cannot readily express how grateful I am to each of you. Sharon is one talented and inspired psychologist and I hope her programs continue not only here but in others prisons. The word is slowly getting out to other wardens just how beneficial these kinds of workshops can be. Time will tell if it has made a difference on the recidivism rate. This will be crucial to getting funding for more programs being available. Other inmates here have shown a great deal of interest in signing up for the other workshops as soon as they are offered."

There was a knock on the office door and Sasha was brought in by one of the new CO's.

"Please come in Sasha and take a seat. Ladies, I want to introduce you to Sasha, the famous ho. Sasha has another job - that of an undercover policewoman. You must never divulge her identity to anyone, including Sharon or your partners. This would put her in a dangerous position. Since this is your last day, we wanted to let you know who our lovely spy is. She will continue on for a short time. She will soon become very ill and will be supposedly transferred to a hospital, where she will receive another assignment. So, if you ever see her again in this capacity, you have to be ready to put on a good act."

"You did an award winning performance. I had a moment of suspicion when you handed me that warning note, but immediately could not believe anyone could be that great of an actress. Meryl Street has nothing on you," pronounced Brooksie.

Lucinda added how she was completely fooled and even felt very sorry for her and her future as a ho.

"Thanks, Sasha, As we planned, the CO is taking you to the doctor's office for the beginning act of your oncoming sickness."

"I would like to offer my thanks," said Sasha. "It has been a privilege, and I can say I really did learn some things about myself that I hadn't been aware of before. I thank you for the great workshops. I honestly believe you have changed the lives of a most of them. Warden, keep an eye on Delores, she has befriended some wild cards and has said a few odd remarks to me. I don't trust her. She has also visited Doc Ronan more times than seemed necessary."

"Thanks again Sasha and I will most definitely heed your warning," answered the Warden. "

As soon as Sasha left, the Warden turned to the four, she shook each one's hand, cleared her throat and thanked them. "I will let you know the final outcome of the investigation when it is over. I'm writing a recommendation an early release for Sharon when her parole hearing comes up. That's not anytime soon, but I believe Sharon will continue to improve the lives of other inmates while she remains here."

After more handshakes, hugs and some tears, the four were escorted out to the gates and Luke was waiting for the pleasure of taking the girls on one of his tours.

CHAPTER THIRTY-NINE

"When you learn, teach; when you get, give."
Maya Angelou (1928-2014)

Houston's day in court.....

Houston who was accompanied by her lawyer, Mr. Lagunta and a guard entered the court room. She was wearing a light blue suit, a white blouse and low heels. She was sporting a new hairdo that flattered her heart shaped face. The blue jacket brought out the blue in her eyes. She appeared calm but was heard taking deep breaths every so often. Mr. Lagunta appeared as dapper as usual. He pulled out a chair for Houston then motioned for her to sit down.

Houston asked him, "Why'd you do tha?. I can move the chair easy enough by myself."

He answered, with a grin, "because you are a lady and I am a gentleman. Get used to it. One day you might actually like polite gestures from men."

"If it hadn't been you pulling out that chair, I woulda thought you were going to hit me over the head with it. That's the sort of men I've been used to. But no more. I kinda like your way."

The court clerk announced, "All rise for Judge Smiley."

Houston's case was first on the docket. It lasted half an hour. She was asked several questions by the judge which she answered to his satisfaction. He spoke to Mr. Lagunta, asked more questions. Then the judge asked the court secretary when was the next available court date for Mr. Lagunta and his client. She gave him a date for three months in to the future. Mr. Lagunta agreed to return with his client at that assigned date.

The three left the court room and walked out of the court house. As soon as they walked to the sidewalk, Houston wrapped her arms around the lawyer and the guard. "I thought I was going to blow up in there, first from fear and then from happiness. I'm going to have a new trial. I believe with all my being that this time it will be fair because you are in my corner Mr. L.. A thousand thanks. You won't be sorry I promise you that.

CHAPTER FORTY

**"It is not the mountain we
conquer, but ourselves."**
Edmund Hillary (1919-2008)

Six months later..............

It was a beautiful fall day, moderate temperature and no rain
in the forecast. The four Social Workers from the Grief Clinic
all were waiting excitedly outside Lancer's Prison to see Houston
emerge a free citizen. The Warden, Dr. Gibran, Mela Washington
and Detectives Yomoto and Rowe were also present. The only
"outsider" was one of Houston's brother who was going to take
her home to his place. He had invited her to live with him. He
also invited Wilamina when she got her walking papers.

"I can only imagine how thrilled Houston must be. Mr.
Lagunta did one fantastic job of representing her case. Rachael,
he is an amazing man and might become a famous lawyer," shared
Brooksie.

"He is an amazing person. Every passing day I learn just how
wonderful he truly is. He is a fighter for the underdog. He deeply
believes in justice for all." responded Rachael. She held her left
hand out for her friends to notice the new, sparkling ring.

Anita exclaimed, "Oh my God, you are going to marry him!
I knew all along how perfect the two of you were for each other.

You've been trying to play down your feelings for him, but I knew he was the one."

"You were right my dear, sweet friend. I was afraid to even dare to think I could love again and be loved in return by such a great man," confessed Rachael.

The group had formed a tight circle around Rachael, voicing their congratulations and complimenting her fiance's taste in jewelry. It was a yellow diamond in an ornate silver setting with a mostly green opal placed to the right of the heart shaped diamond.

Just then, they could hear the gates opening and the first one to spot Houston was Mela, her heart was racing. "Hey Tex, over here. We are your welcoming committee. We tried to get a band and they would be playing the 'Yellow Rose of Texas', but no luck." Everyone raced over to the new releasee who appeared in shock. Houston had stopped in midstride with her mouth wide open. Her eyes started to sparkle and she opened her arms out wide to hug the wave of supporters.

"I can't believe you're all here just for me. Wow!"

Joyful tears were flowing from all participants. Good wishes, good luck and good-byes were in abundance. Houston's brother had been waiting by his car and eventually she spotted him. She waved enthusiastically towards him and after a few more hugs she left with her brother to start her new life.

Brooksie gave her a day planner, in which she had written in a date for two weeks hence to meet at the Table Talk Cafe to talk about Houston's plans for the agency. It was the understanding that Wilamina would be released soon after the new year and then their business plan could become a reality. Brooksie located a small office a few blocks away from the Grief Clinic and was anxious to show it to Houston. It needed some sprucing up and some minor repairs which Luke and Tony offered to do. It was affordable and in a good location. The owner of the run down office was willing to take a small deposit to hold the office for several months. He had been trying to rent it for a long time so the rent was dirt cheap. He was just glad to finally have a renter who will move in at a later date.

CHAPTER FORTY-ONE

**"One who walks in another's tracks
leaves no footprints."**
Italian Proverb

One year later.........

A great deal has transpired for the Grief Clinic's social workers, for several of the inmates of Lancer's Prison and for many of the staff. For some folks, it was terrific and for others, not so great.

Dr. Ronan was arrested for selling a variety of drugs to inmates, to prison guards and to several others outside the prison walls. He is facing some serious prison time. He is out on bail at present, no longer employed at the prison or anywhere else for that matter. His MD license may soon be revoked. A boatload of evidence is being gathered regarding his sexual abuse of mostly young inmates. Mrs. Ronan has filed for divorce and has expressed plans to 'leave the piece of shit' with zero assets. His nurse has kept her word and is singing like a magpie about the doctor and the Warden's assistant.

Janet Black, the doctor's long time nurse, has been very cooperative with the police and has turned over damaging evidence against Dr. Ronan. She had been keeping records of the missing drugs and the substitution of placeboes for the narcotics given to inmates. Her own blackmail scheme of the doctor and the assistant warden was also exposed. Janet's financial problems will soon be in the past, as she will probably become a resident of Lancer's Prison.

Malina, was fired from her position at the prison and numerous complaints have been filed against her by inmates. They are stating that she was well aware of the sexual intimidation by Dr. Ronan and was also aware of the pain medications being watered down or not given at all to patients. Her husband has filed for divorce and the R.N. licensing board is reviewing her status.

More evidence against Malina is surfacing slowly. She continues to deny she instructed her husband to run the facilitator's car off the road. It seems it is his word against hers. She remains free at the present time, but her future looks bleak. She has coveted the Warden's job for years and they say no way will she ever work again at any prison. She may eventually find herself on the other side of the prison bars.

Bo Smithers was found guilty of hit and run, given three years jail time and ten years probation. He cooperated with the detectives and helped them and the prosecutor of Dr. Ronan and his wife, Malina.

Sasha, the plant and cell mate of Maxine Ritter, gathered enough damaging information against Maxine and Rank Johnson to guarantee both would continue to be locked up and tried for the murder of Simone.

The Warden continues to be in charge of Lancers. She has learned a great deal and puts her new knowledge to work daily to improve conditions and goals for inmates and COs. The prison offers the twelve workshops all during the year. There is soon to be a number of workshops for the guards as well. The Warden has been asked to give presentations, along with several of the Grief Clinic social workers to prisons around the country.

The dog training project that uses inmates is in full swing. Brooksie's Aunt Tilly continues to be the go-between for the animal shelters who furnish the prison with dogs appropriate to be trained for various duties.

The prison's new assistant has been in charge of keeping the stats on the recidivism rate for the past year. So far it shows a drop of 3% since the workshops have been made available. This is considered success and hopefully will show a higher percent in the near future.

Delores, an inmate and one of the members of Brooksie and Lucinda's group, was discovered to be helping Malina and Maxine Ritter. She was gathering information with the purpose of causing harm to the facilitators, to Sharon and to the Warden. When she was confronted she confessed to aiding Dr. Ronan. He paid her with drugs to feed her addiction. She also aided the assistant warden by slipping her information about the route the facilitators took to get to and from the prison. She had also been privy to the plan to kill Simone and Sharon. She turned out to be a treasure trove of information for the police.

After the release of Houston and more recently the release of Wilamina, they opened their door for business. Their very first client was sent to them by their friends from the Grief Clinic.

Many of the inmates who attended the six month workshops kept in touch with the social workers mostly by mail, and once in a while by phone. The Warden is also a continuing source of follow up information, by keeping the communication lines open between them. She makes it a point to keep herself abreast of how the inmates are doing after attending the workshops, with those who have been or will be released.

The Detectives Yomoto and Rowe have remained friends with Warden James and the four social workers. They don't see each other often, but make it a point to get together every few months.

They have both become Sharon's regular visitors. Mutual respect is the glue and the detectives plan to be present at Sharon's first parole hearing. She has some influential friends on her side which can only help her. Sharon is again writing books and programs for the addicted and incarcerated. She continues to be a great role model and listening post for those around her.

CHAPTER FORTY-TWO

**"...friendship, the ease of it, it is not something
to be taken lightly - nor for
granted. Because, after
breathing and eating and
sleeping, friendships are
essential to our survival."**
Adelaide Bry

Facilitators lunch date..........

Brooksie and the other three social workers are planning to continue offering support groups at the clinic. She and her co-workers have been invited to facilitate workshops at Lancers, as volunteers again. Sharon has offered to be a co-facilitator if needed. Attorney Lagunta has been busy working on getting her sentence reduced. Sharon continues to write books and programs. Her purpose is to encourage, inspire and educate inmates so that when they are released how to wisely use their time. The workshops encourage them to take advantage of all the courses that are offered in prison. The goal is to encourage learning skills, and to help them find their own callings which requires the development of character.

"Here we go again my friends," expressed Brooksie with a smile. "Since we have all agreed to help Sharon out again to facilitate another six months of workshops, I suggest we drive together twice month We should combine our time and day to still split the groups, to ten in each. At least this won't be for safety reasons. We will save gas and have more time to visit. We could take turns driving our own car or not."

"I like your suggestions and I would love to show off my new Suburban," offered Rachael. A surprise gift from my darling intended. Roco really enjoys gift giving to many. He especially enjoys surprising someone. I'm so not used to such generosity, but I'm learning to love it."

Anita and Lucinda both said they couldn't go to Lancers twice a month, but could make it once a month.

"That's no problem," answered Brooksie. Sharon has already offered to be co-facilitator whenever we need her. I think she would love the chance to sit in and participate. Rachael, you and I can work the same group. Anita and Sharon take the other ten women one week and the next week Lucinda and Sharon work with the same women. That way Sharon will always be with the same ten people. It will offer consistency."

"We can work out the details later. Now I'd like to get to more personal things. Roco and I have are working on a date to get hitched. Just want to make sure you'll all be available. We are considering a weekend in the middle of July. How does that fit with you three?"

All gave positive nods. Anita shared her joy for all and teased the girls about an announcement she might soon be making regarding her own boyfriend.

Brooksie and Luke had been already been married for three months. The marriage party had included Brooksie's best friends, the three social workers and their partners or dates. Luke's parents brought his adopted son, Drake and soon to be sister, the three year old foster child of the newly married couple. The adoption process is in the beginning stages. Aunt Tilly, Uncle Joe, Houston, Wilamina and Sammy (recently released), Dr. Blackmore, Warden James, Detectives Yomoto and Rowe, and lastly Sasha, who has given up undercover work and is now a homicide detective. Dr. Sharon Primm attended with the help of skype. The wedding took place at Brooksie's home. There were all of Brooksies' four legged critters in the wedding party. They were a noisy bunch of excited pets. The reception was later held at Luke's home. Luke, Brooksie, Drake and their soon to be adopted daughter, Joy are residing at Luke's fine home. Aunt Tilly has gleefuly added to their menagerie, one crippled puppy and one three legged cat.

Uncle Joe and Aunt Tilly now have a dinner one Sunday a month for their niece, Brooksie, her husband Luke and his parents, including Drake and his soon to be adopted sister, Joy.

Look for my next book

Salt and Pepper Detective Agency

A MYSTERY NOVEL

Donna Underwood

ABOUT THE AUTHOR

Donna Underwood is a retired nurse who has been involved in grief work for the past twenty plus years. She is the author of three nonfiction books on grief and three fictional mysteries. She is working on a fourth mystery novel. She lives in Kennewick, WA with her husband Wayne, and two dogs and five cats.

Printed in the United States
By Bookmasters